Dance OF DUALITY

A story of a Soul Blossoming

VINITA PANDE

notionpress.com

INDIA · SINGAPORE · MALAYSIA

ISBN 979-8-89498-857-3

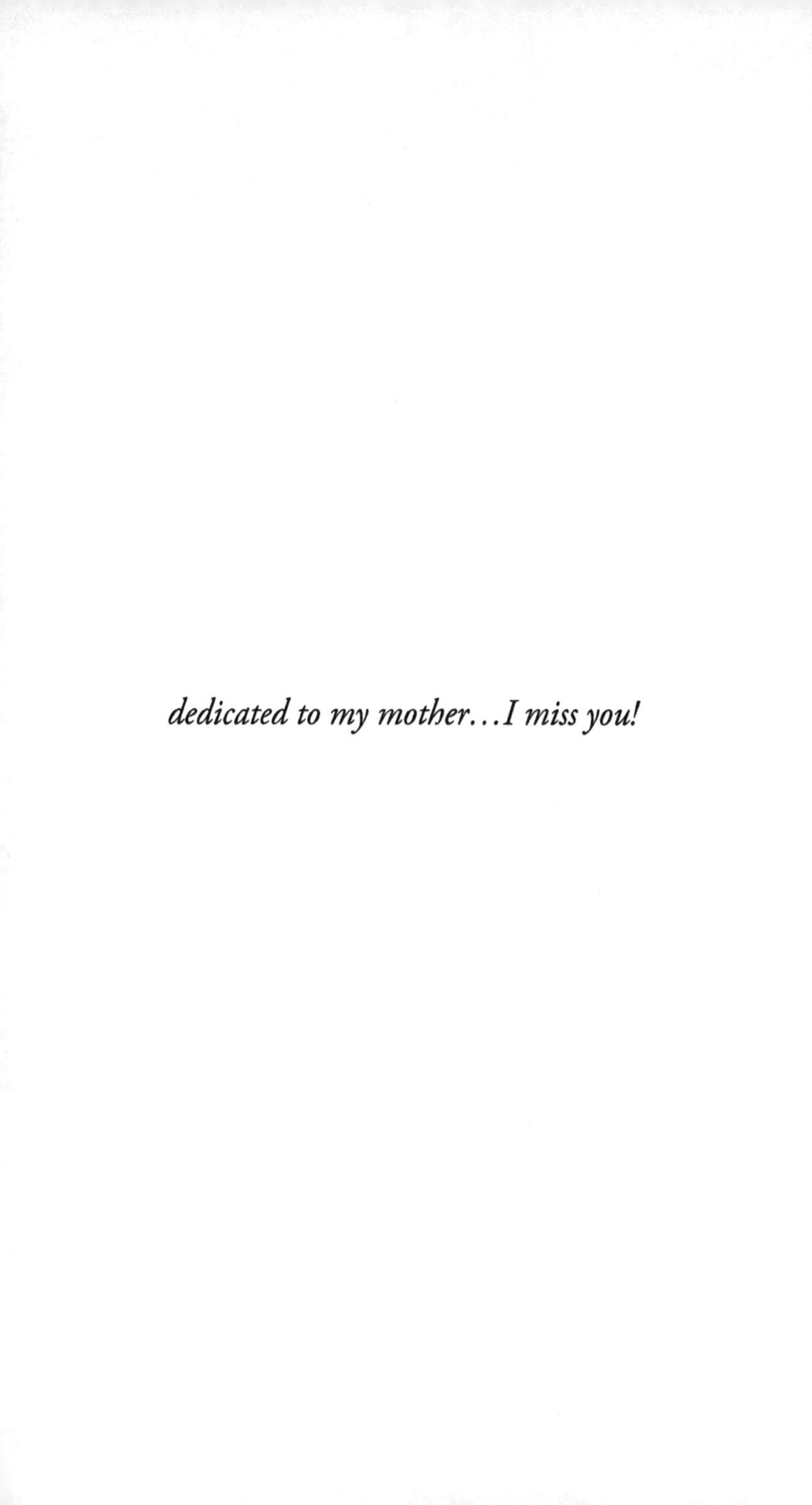

dedicated to my mother…I miss you!

Contents

Preface

This novel is an unusual life story about a Kashmiri woman named Lalla. Supernatural at times and ordinary otherwise, this fictional tale also borrows experiences from the author's own life. Born into a Kashmiri family, Lalla is named after the famous Kashmiri mystic, Lal Ded (pronounced *Deadh*, meaning grandmother), also known as Lalleshwari. She has a twin brother, Abhi, named in honor of the legendary Kashmiri Shaivism master, Abhinavagupta. These two souls choose their divergent life paths as an exposition of duality, of light and darkness, positive and negative, evolutionary and destructive. Lalla discovers her life's purpose to integrate the spiritual into the worldly, by experiencing, understanding and overcoming human problems in order to help others with their issues. Some extraordinary spiritual experiences are woven into the fabric of a pragmatic life, often unbeknownst to Lalla's family and friends.

The story starts with her soul in a heavenly dimension where souls reside, and also ends in a realm beyond the physical earth plane. Lalla and her twin are born in Kashmir and later move to the capital

New Delhi. As she moves through a more traditional path, she gets married to another Kashmiri who lives and works in the San Francisco Bay Area. Readers will be able to relate some events in the story which are from the past and present, like COVID.

Many amazing, mystical phenomena are described, especially as the tale pivots from events we have already experienced like COVID, into the future yet to come. The story is truly about the chrysalis of a soul's evolution and blossoming into a new form. A Self's expression through the human experience, and a dance with duality to find non-duality. Those who master both, win the game.

Summary

(Chapter 1) The story starts with her soul in a heavenly dimension where souls reside, and states the purpose of her soul's incarnation on the planet at this time.

(Chapter 2) Lalla and her twin are then born in Srinagar, Kashmir, where they enjoy the bliss of early childhood. The narration describes the subtle realm that overlays the physical world, while moving through a very relatable storyline.

(Chapter 3) When Lalla is still a child the family move to the capital New Delhi where her father works as a surgeon. Lalla is different from other children, and has transformational mystical experiences even as a young teenager. Her twin brother is a stark contrast from her in how notorious he is. College is a cultural shift for a naive Lalla who adjusts and then thrives with college friendships.

(Chapter 4) In between college and starting a career, Lalla pursues her longing to be in a spiritual environment and attends a summer course in Rishikesh (in the Himalayas). This escapade gives her a glimpse into the manifestation from the alignment of her inner and outer worlds.

(Chapter 5) As she chooses to also pursue a worldly life and follow a traditional path, she starts working, and is later introduced to a Kashmiri boy who works in the San Francisco Bay Area. Their courtship defines an ideal supportive relationship, and later they are married in a traditional Kashmiri wedding.

(Chapter 6) Her twin brother goes through a breakup while she enters a model married life in the Bay Area. Even though her husband Sid is not spiritual like her, they share a bond of love and respect for each other. While she is engaged in her new married life, Lalla's spiritual life takes a back seat.

(Chapter 7) Readers will be able to relate to some events in the story which are from the past and present, like the Kashmiri Pandits' exodus. This becomes a life changing event for her. Seeing the injustice and suffering of the Pandits, thrusts her back to align with her spiritual purpose.

(Chapter 8) Lalla chanced upon a famous channel-medium while watching a TV program on past lives. She immediately signs up for a session with this channeler which opens the doors into the amazing world of new age spirituality. Abhi comes to California to visit Lalla and Sid and mocks Lalla's new age pursuits in front of her husband to rock her self-confidence and bring doubt in her.

(Chapter 9) Even though her life is becoming more spiritual, she fully integrates her spiritual awakening into practical life, which she feels is her life purpose. Her husband Sid is always an understanding and supportive partner. Going deeper into the mystical, she not only takes a past life regression (PLR) session, she becomes a PLR therapist. In the meantime, her twin brother finally gets married to a very nice Kashmiri girl. Abhi insults Lalla in front of the family again but this time her confidence is not shattered.

(Chapter 10) Lalla's seeking for a Guru is fulfilled when she finds a spiritual master Sri M. She and Sid attend a workshop where they are initiated into Kriya Yoga. She experiences many things in the astral realm related to Sri M, who is a great master like Yogananda.

(Chapter 11) Shortly after a revelational experience during a spiritual session on 'Life Between Lives', COVID hits the world. Unfortunately, Dr. Sid catches COVID, becomes critical and will he die? Lalla discovers what phenomenon took place which is astounding and unusual.

(Chapter 12) Shocking at first, she later adjusts to this predestined event. After COVID Lalla starts to counsel and heal many people in her network of friends. All along there is an interlacing of the spiritual with the worldly.

(Chapter 13) Many amazing, mystical phenomena are described, especially as the tale pivots into what we can consider the future. There are social issues discussed and spiritual knowledge infused into the narration. Lalla now evolves into a channel as more and more of higher consciousness flows through her, while the world enters a transition phase of major wars and natural disasters.

(Chapter 14) The narration about what's yet to come includes major changes in financial systems, severe effects to the economy and life in cities from conflicts and catastrophes. With many self-sustaining communities sprouting around the world, Lalla decides to move to one such community in Colorado. While the community blossoms with super-human abilities, there is a split in humanity between the spiritual and physical, and the material world starts degenerating. This contrast is exhibited in the lives of Lalla and her twin Abhi.

(Chapter 15) There are three waves of solar flares which carry magical downloads from a higher consciousness that descends on those purified to receive. The shift of the planet and humanity into a new age describe a new race of light beings, and Lalla fulfills her purpose of coming to the planet at this time. Some aspects of the conclusion resonate with messages conveyed by aspirants of the new age spirituality.

Chapter 1

Sliding on Bridges of Light

In my soul's divine home there is only bliss. We are free beings floating and flying as we wish in another mansion of creation. Although we don't have physical bodies, we can see without eyes, hear without ears, and speak without tongues. Communication is telepathic, and knowledge is coded in light - subtle light that is. There are no limits or boundaries, and nothing is hidden or unknown. Things manifest the moment we intend them. Existence is effortless. There is peace. Everything flows and functions according to natural laws and comic order, also known as *Dharm*.

Here, in the realm of souls, my name is *Keev* and my nature is like that of an innocent child who loves knowledge. I chose this combination to be wise yet childlike. If I were only like a child, I may remain childish, and if I only had knowledge, I could become arrogant. So, I enjoyed the depths of knowledge with joy. In this higher realm we experience subtle feelings like love, but not negative ones like fear, anger or attachment.

My being belonged to a group of twelve souls, and we were born like litter from the Cosmic Divine Mother's womb ages ago. We evolved together by expressing our inner potential, incarnating in various forms in creation, gathering experiences from many planets in many dimensions. Then we integrated those experiences to transform and evolve. Some in our group evolved faster than the rest of us and moved on to other soul groups where they continued their evolution.

My soul family is now a group of eight. All of us are energetically connected as one entity, yet we maintain our uniqueness. Our souls can be seen as energy or light forms that are linked together in an octagonal shape. Similar to the structure of a molecule. Each group of souls holds some speciality and many of these groups put together make up a function of creation. Synonymous to groups of cells which make up an organ or a system in a body. My soul family specializes in vibrations, we are like vibrational doctors. Soul groups get guidance and direction from masters who are more evolved. Like recently we got direction from messenger beings, that went from group to group, telling us to send higher vibrations down to a planet called Earth. Since then, we have been sending our vibrational energy to Earth which descends like a waterfall through the center of our group. There must be some bigger plan ordained by masters in higher realms, the details of which are unknown to us.

We have learnt from many beings, like *Gurus, Devas, Siddhas, Rishis, Avatars*, angels, and many ascended masters like Jesus. Here Jesus is known as *Sanat Kumar*, a son of the creator being *Brahma*. Depending on what we need, and what we are ready for, a master with that specialization comes to help us. Knowledge is given with the blessings of a master, transferred by either a divine touch, divine light or just energy. If I look up from where I am with my soul family, it's like looking up from the depths of an ocean, seeing many groups of ocean beings floating across. There are a myriad of higher beings of different races, each with their functions in maintaining creation. In the Vedic tradition these beings are called *Devas*, or light beings. At the topmost center of this giant ocean is a brilliant light shining more brilliantly than any star. We know this as the Source or Supreme Being. From this Source layers of creation have manifested. Some of the highest beings merged into Source, though most beings remain in existence to fulfill their functions or role in creation.

We knew most of the great masters in these higher realms. We were aware of their roles and interacted with them. Once a master appeared before me, he wore a crown, had a beard, and looked deep into me. A moment later he touched my third eye, between the eyebrows, and I felt completely immersed in trance. I felt a blissful energy entering my forehead and flowing down into my heart and invigorating my whole being. He conveyed to me telepathically that the abilities and knowledge transferred to me were needed for the next level of my evolution. It was a pleasant experience and I felt elated.

Though there is no earthly sense of time, things happen on a much larger scale, and there is some sequence to it. We are not bound, and we can skip forward or backward in events as needed. Life here is magical. I was happy, flying around like a kid in my familiar neighborhood, sliding on bridges of light, experimenting with manifestations from consciousness. Elders were busy with their duties, the Masters were engrossed in the maintenance of existence according to *Dharm*.

I also went on missions as and when needed. Once there was a planet whose vibrations and electromagnetic field had gone out of balance, and I heard a mental call for help. Traveling in non-physical realms is through intent. As soon as you intend to go somewhere, you move there almost instantaneously. It is faster than the speed of light.

As I rushed to this planet, I flew out of the boundary of my realm, into a different density of another realm, it is like flying through thin air and then diving into an ocean which is denser. It was a white planet which looked almost like a space station with the core made of diagonal white lattice. As I flew in and landed in my subtle body that looked translucent with white glowing outline. I met with the person who had called me (telepathically), he had a denser, more solid body. This simple sweet man who was rather distraught right now being the engineer in charge of the planet's controlling mechanism. He was at the north pole of the planet from where the magnetic and vibrational field of the planet was controlled. We walked into a giant pyramid, and then walked up many flights of steps through a dark corridor till we reached a large cavity. At the center of this chamber was a large instrumentation of magnificent crystals.

"These crystals stopped conducting energy somehow, and I couldn't re-ignite them with the energy jump as I've done in the past. I didn't know what else to do, so I called for help," he explained, looking very worried.

The functioning of the crystals which controlled the energy of the planet. I repaired or healed these crystals by sending vibrations of the correct frequencies from my own energy. He watched the light rays of energy being transmitted from me to the crystals. The instrumentation re-attuned and brought the planet back into balance. Taking a sigh of relief, the caretaker smiled looking at the restored functioning of energy crystals and thanked me profusely. I too felt fulfilled to be able to help all these beings here and then bid farewell. Then I flew out and away from the planet, halted and turned towards it to send blessings of light that engulfed the entire planet. It felt so much better!

Almost instantaneously I was back in my realm, to my soul family. There was someone here waiting for me. He approached me with some urgency. He was one of messengers of *Sri Vishnu.* Apparently, there was a great need for volunteers to manifest on a planet that is going to go through a big transformation. This would require a lot of energy and those who specialize in higher vibrations would be best suited for this mission. It is for this reason that my soul family was transmitting higher vibrations to Gaia (Earth). There were several waves of souls that were going, and I would go with one of the waves going there to help. As my soul had incarnated on this planet several times, I would be a good candidate to go back. It appeared as though he was pleading with me. But I wasn't convinced, "*Why me?*" Besides, my soul didn't feel the calling to send a ray of myself on this tough, uncomfortable mission. I did some introspection to see what my inner vision revealed. I sensed that I had some unfinished business still to clear, and I was to be a part of *Vishnu's* army of souls that had to go on this divine mission.

For my next incarnation I was given guidance by one of the elders (guides) on which life and family to choose, which experiences to gather, what purpose to serve, and so on. There was a prospective body that was going to be born with the suitable DNA for my soul. The life path of this human being was shown to me like a trailer of a movie with its major milestones. So, the chapters of my next life were drafted. Once this was envisioned, the group of souls who were to be my family, along with some others, were brought into a gathering area. This was like a director's conference room, where the main characters of a drama were gathered to discuss the script to be enacted. It also aligned with what guidance I had just received for my next birth.

Some of us had unresolved matters, *Karm*, from previous births together. *Karm* is like undissipated energy that needs to be consumed. When we do not act according to *Dharm* we create *Karm*. It's just a way for the creator to create a drama, for souls to experience and learn. If everything was perfect and we didn't experiment, what would be the point of creation? It would be like a blank script for a play. So the next act for the play was being written by the guides as our directors and our group of souls as actors. We picked a syllabus for this next life, a lesson plan, and selected the *Karm* we were going to work on with each other's help. For example, the soul who was going to be my twin brother was a narcissist in a previous birth. In the upcoming birth a similar pattern would repeat and the soul of his wife-to-be is volunteering to help him learn this lesson this time and evolve. This was going to be a Karmic marriage, like most marriages are. They serve a purpose. We learn the most from relationships. I too chose to have a marriage chapter in my life sketch, something I had neglected or escaped from in a previous life. Most of my family, and my to-be husband's family would take rebirth in the same roles we held last time, to recreate this act and improve from last time.

While we are souls there is no animosity or negativity, it's neutral, the drama of emotions is only on the planet. There are no positive or negative experiences from a soul's perspective because all experiences are for the soul's learning. With guidance from our masters, we talked about who plays what role in our next lives together. As an example, a soul who was my husband in a previous life was going to be my son, so I can give him unconditional love this time through the difficulties we encounter. It is very interesting that the stars under which we are born amazingly line up with the life plan and *Karm* we have chosen.

Most of us had spent several lives together, and many of us had some unresolved *Karm*, though not all. Some souls were coming on the journey as supportive souls, as many of us were going to hold the space for the other to evolve together. One of these souls, *Reev*, was a close buddy of mine, we had explored many realms and life experiences together. We both had an adventurous nature, having fun and excitement while we learnt for huge leaps of soul evolution. This time we came up with a partnership on a very interesting storyline, and one that was pertinent for this planet's current timeline. We, *Reev* and *Keev,* decided to be born as twins, brother and sister. He volunteered to embody fear and all the forms it takes, while I would exemplify divine love. This would showcase the contrast to humanity, that fear is self-destructive, and love is clearly the path for our survival. It was critical at this juncture for humans to step up to the higher vibration of love, as the planet itself was moving to higher vibrations. Love and fear are the duality of the divine in creation, and therefore we were going to embody these as divine twins!

We were ready and it was now time to descend one by one to Gaia. We didn't have to wait long for our parents to be born and married to then be born to them. There is a mystery on how souls descend and merge into the womb. It is a delicate task and there are specialist souls who have mastered this technique. These angelic beings took my to-be twin and I to a preparatory staging area where we were ready to go down to the vibrations of the earth which are far denser and heavier. An etheric shield was put around us, the chakras were attuned, and some adjustments were made to our subtle bodies. With these light beings on either side of us, both of us started descending down a vortex of light. The planet became visible below, coming closer and closer, and suddenly we went into a deep slumber. A veil was put over all our knowledge, and amnesia set in so we couldn't remember anything about our true identities.

As I entered the fetus in the womb, there was an immense constriction from the vast expanse of the soul into a very small, limited body. We had entered our mother's womb just before birth. Souls can enter anytime from the fifth month to before delivery. My mother's energy felt so immensely loving and gentle, I made an instant connection with her. The next thing we experienced was being pushed out to be born. I went first. From the contractions inside the small dark space, filled with warm fluid, I popped out into a very bright cold room with the loud voices of the nurses and a lady gynecologist who picked me up. A few mins later out came my twin brother, and everyone was jubilant. There was much celebration, and my poor mom was exhausted.

And so our next story on this beautiful planet began!

Chapter 2

A Child Arrives in the World

Once long ago my soul was born from the Cosmic Mother, in a similar way my human incarnation was now born from a human mother. It is so difficult for a soul to descend into the dense vibrations and gravity of the Earth. Initially, I, the soul, spent a lot of time out of the body in astral realms for long hours while I, the baby slept. This made it easy for my soul to slowly adapt to its new garment, a human body. When the body's base needs for food and poop were needed, the baby cried, though the nature of the female body I had adopted was quite calm. My twin brother, however, whose soul was playing the role of fear in this life, cried often and was difficult to breastfeed. My gentle and loving mother's caress and cradling was so blissful. I was happy to have her back as my mom, as in one of my previous lives she had died due to an ectopic pregnancy when I was just a child. The impression of that pain of losing my mother's unconditional love was still with me. Now I was in her arms again. My mother was like an expression of the Divine Mother herself. My dynamic and high energy father (who was also my father in the same past life) came to check on my mother and picked me up from the cradle. He smiled at me, kissed me, and spoke to me in baby language. I could barely see anything from my physical eyes, but I felt everything, and knew many things intuitively, as most babies do.

My twin brother was in another cradle next to mine. My strong and firm aunt was holding him, with my gentle paternal uncle (my father's older brother) looking on. It was the mid-60s on the planet, in the month of September and so much was happening around the world. I was born into a Kashmiri Pandit family in Srinagar, India, a turbulent part of the country which was relatively stable when I was born. My father, SadaShiv Bhatt, was a surgeon, working in the medical university hospital where we were born. He was a brave, positive minded, 007 type personality. My parents had recently returned from England where my father studied and worked as a surgeon after leaving his elite family business in Kashmir. It had been nine long years of my parents trying for a child, my soft and beautiful mother, Sharada, was given fertility pills, and now they had twins.

We stayed in the hospital for five days, after which we moved to our new home. My parents, uncle, and aunt, lived in a beautiful wooden bungalow on the north side of the famous Dal Lake of Srinagar. The house staff was so happy to see us as they opened the gate to our long driveway. Autumn was setting in, leaves were turning colors and falling from the trees in our picturesque yard. As we exited the car, my father picked me up from my mother's lap. I could feel the cool air for the first time. I was well bundled in a hand knitted soft wool jersey, cap and booties. Our nanny, whom everyone called Gonna Deadh ('deadh' is used for a grandmother type figure), was standing at the entryway with others to honor our first entry into our home. She held a plate with a lit oil lamp, some flowers, rice, and a paste of saffron mixed with chandan which she put on our foreheads with her ring finger. The air in the house was pleasant with the subtle scent of Deodar and walnut wood. Gonna Deadh told my mother that the parent's room had been prepared and kept warm, so we headed upstairs to our cozy room. My twin brother and I were nursed and went to sleep. My mother could also rest now.

Unbeknownst to anyone except my twin and I, several family members who had passed on came to see the newborns and celebrate. It is joyous for them as well. This included our great grandfather, and grandparents from both sides of the family. There were also some Kashmiri spiritual masters who came in their etheric bodies that had connections to our family, as well as our guides for this life. These guides were already giving us messages and knowledge pertinent for our days ahead. My twin and

I also had long telepathic conversations at the soul level and shared our experiences of this new life.

The next day, the sixth day from our birth, we were given a herbal purifying bath, which is one of life's milestone rituals, *Samskāras*, in the Vedic tradition. In the old days the umbilical cord was partially left and it dried and fell off naturally, after which this bath was given. Perhaps common in other native traditions as well. Then on the eleventh day is another important milestone, in Kashmiris it's called *Kah Naethar,* commonly known in Sanskrit as the *Naam Karan* ceremony, somewhat like baptism, where we are given our names. The older family members wanted to follow the ancient tradition of naming us according to our birth star, *Nakshatra*. This tradition had been lost for several generations but now they wanted to revive it. Each constellation has two or three prominent or ruling stars, which totals twenty seven (27) *Nakshatras*. Vedic philosophy says that each object has a resonant frequency and so also each *Nakshatra* is associated with a letter sound. This sound vibration resonates with the souls that are born under its influence. Therefore when we call a person by the name that starts with this sound it has a harmonizing effect on the soul. Interestingly, my twin and I were born forty minutes apart, so we were born under different *Nakshatras*.

Many extended family members, neighbors, and close friends had come for our *Kah Naethar* ceremony.

Many masters, divine beings and ancestors were also present at the ceremony in their astral forms. Our *Kul Brahmin* (priest), Prakash Boi, came late and started the ceremony immediately. He had created our birth charts according to *Jyotish*, Vedic astrology, and wrote our names according to our *Nakshatras*. These were names that we as souls had chosen, though as the drama plays out we are not aware of these higher truths. My twin brother was given the name, Abhinava, to be called Abhi for short. Abhinavagupta was a famous Kashmiri Shaivism philosopher, a mystic and aesthetician from the tenth century in Kashmir. He was also considered an influential musician, poet, dramatist, exegete, theologian, and logician.

I was given the name Lalleshwari, or Lalla for short, which was also the name of a famous mystic saint of Kashmir from the fourteenth century, venerated by both Hindus and Muslims over the centuries. Lalleshwari, commonly known as Lal Ded (pronounced *Deadh*, meaning grandmother), used to spontaneously sing poems of deep mystical knowledge, known as *Vakhs*. She was an existential presence of Kashmiri Shaivism, a saint who had merged with the Source.

The scent of the offerings in the prayer, flowers, camphor, *ghee* lamp, filled the room and purified the environment. An earthen pot woven around with a wicker filled with hot embers, called *Kanger*, was prepared by the priest, then given to my older aunt. She took seeds out from a linen pouch, touched both Sid's shoulders and forehead, then offered them into the *Kanger* to burn. She repeated this with me, and both our parents. There can be no celebration in India without food! It was the first event after our birth, and that too after so many years of waiting for a child, so the celebrations were grand. Many Kashmiri delicacies were prepared for the feast called *Saal*. We as babies were tired and were taken by Gonna Deadh upstairs to be cradled to sleep while the elders engaged in vibrant conversations downstairs. After everyone left, the dozen or so house staff also ate, and our family sat together talking over Kashmiri tea, Kashmiri *kehva,* discussing family and friends who came.

Our childhood was spent in utter bliss, much like heaven, in the shadow of the grand Himalayas, the beauty of the Kashmir valley, crisp clean air, open spaces to run and have fun, and be nurtured by our extended family. Occasionally we had *Pujas* and *Abhishek* at home to honor the great One undivided consciousness, *Rudra* or *Shiva* in Kashmiri Shaivism. We also had *pujas* for *Narayan* the primordial Being in the *Vaishnav* tradition of our ancestors. On one such occasion when we were four, there was an elaborate *puja* at our home. *Sanskrit* chanting was going on, and the room was filled with the scent of incense, camphor, *ghee,* and flowers. I remembered this fragrance and the feeling of these sacred offerings for the rest of my life. However, Abhi was agitated and restless. He was usually hyper and couldn't sit still, even though my mother tried to talk him into sitting quietly. He threw a tantrum and left the room. I; however, I couldn't keep my eyes open. My mind was absorbed in the vibrations of the *Mantras* and I slowly drifted into a deep trance, to be later awoken by a cousin tapping on my shoulder to hand me some *Prasaad* (similar to the wine and bread given at the end of a Catholic Mass). My aunt was singing a *Bhajan* while playing the harmonium, my mother chimed the cymbals, and the *Brahmin*, Prakash Boi, rang the prayer bell while chanting some *Mantras* to conclude the *Puja*.

Then I saw a saint-like person, a translucent figure, walk down the middle aisle in the room blessing people on both sides with his right hand and smiling. I was neither shocked nor scared, I was in a different state of awareness, one in which I seemed to have a 'knowing'. I did not realize that no one else could see him except me, and at that young age I could not differentiate between what was normal vs. mystical. That recognition came later when I grew up. When he disappeared after blessing everyone I saw the clock on the back wall, the time was 11:11am.

Many years later I realized that the saint that appeared was Bhatt Kalshar. He was one of our family's forefathers, and his portrait was in our *Puja* room. Bhatt

Kalshar was famous for the hymns he channeled that were written into the Sikh text, the *Adi Granth*. This was at the time of Guru Arjan Dev, in the latter half of the 16th century. He brought along with him ten other Kashmiri Pandit Bhatts to be with Guru Arjan. All eleven of these Bhatts composed hymns that were incorporated into the *Adi Granth*, which later became the *Guru Granth Sahib*. One third of the *Granth* is from the contributions of these Bhatts. One of the common phrases in Sikhism, '*Wahe Guru*' was actually introduced by Bhatt Gayand ji, as it's a common term in Kashmiri Shaivism.

"Zainab!" I yelled running, slipping and sliding in my slippers, "wait for me".

Zainab, my five year old classmate and best friend, ran ahead of me laughing. She ran right through the entrance of her modest home and hid behind the door. Her father, Ali, stood there watching us.

I came inside and asked, "Salaam uncle, have you seen Zainab?"

He just smiled.

Hussain, her seven year old brother, stormed into the room and pulled Zainab out from behind the door, producing her in front of me saying, "here she is Lalla".

"Stop it Hussain! Leave my hand!"

Zainab broke her hand free from his grab and said, "*Chalo* Lalla, let's go upstairs".

"Wait Zainab," said aunty from inside the kitchen, "eat something first".

Four older brothers of Zainab returned from the *Madrassa*, the Islamic study school where they went. We all sat around the long wooden table, Zainab's six siblings, father, and us. Aunty and Zainab's elder sister served us food and almond blossom colored milk tea, called *Sheer chai*. Both of us were in our own world talking about what we would play next while the older siblings and uncle were discussing more serious affairs.

Just then, two very intense looking men, uncle's friend and son, came to pay a visit. They were greeted, asked to join us on the table, then served tea and food. Once we finished the elders were moving to the living room area, while Zainab and I were heading upstairs.

The young man who had come with his father stared down at me, then suddenly put his hand forcefully on my shoulder saying, "Eh, she's a Kafir! Why do you have her as your friend?"

I froze with shock.

Hussain immediately intervened, removing his hand off my shoulder saying, "She's not a Kafir! And it's none of your business!"

Young Hussain stared daringly at the much taller and muscular young man. Both the fathers stepped in and de-escalated the situation. While my heart was pounding and my mind numb with fright, Zainab pulled me towards her and embraced me in her arms. My hands and feet were trembling. I felt too uncomfortable to stay, so I moved away from Zainab, and ran out of the house.

Our driver was standing at a distance, "Rehman joo", I yelled, "*Chalo* - let's go!"

I opened the back door of the car and sat inside panting.

"What happened, Lalla?" Rehman asked.

"Nothing, I just want to go home now," I said.

When I reached home and entered, I saw Abhi sprawling on the floor in the corridor crying and yelling at the top of his voice, "Nooo! I want that truck!"

He was hysterical about getting a toy he had seen. Big crocodile tears on his red fuming face, his fringe haircut bothering his eyes, and banging his fists on the wall and floor.

"Abhi! We just got you a big toy car last week. Now come here and eat," my mother tried to reason with him.

It was too much for her to handle. Then she went into a bedroom where my aunt sat and murmured something to her. My aunt came out, bent down, and whispered something into Abhi's ears.

Instantly, Abhi's eyes lit up, and with a bright smile on his face he nodded like a tamed animal, "Yeah! I want, I want!"

Seemed like my aunt had bribed him with something, again. *Such a cunning little monster you are Abhi,* I thought. I couldn't care less, I was tired and sad, and went running to Gonna Deadh in the kitchen and clung to her *Sari,* almost in tears.

"Oh! what happened, Lalla?" she asked, bending down and looking into my eyes with concern. I put my arms around her neck and leaned into her.

She picked me up and then placed me on the kitchen counter, worried, she kept asking, "Did someone do something to you? Or hurt you? Huh? You can tell me."

Tears rolled down my cheeks and she wiped them with the end of her *Sari.*

"Some people at Zainab's home were very mean to me," I said, sobbing.

"Never mind them. People are always saying things good and bad, it's just words. They are bad for saying it, so why should you feel bad? I'm there no? Don't worry. Ok? Here, have some lemonade".

That night, in my sleep, as I shot up into the astral realms, like we all do, I was joined by my spirit guides in long flowy white robes and light bodies. There also were the souls of Hussain, Zainab and Wahab, the young man who had called me '*Kafir*', a non-believer of Islam. Here however, we did not have those identities of man made religions or their beliefs used to control humans for power. There are universal laws here, and no one can deny the truth or true reality. The lives we were living on the planet were like a dream, like a movie which we saw from here together with our guides, while we slept in our beds on earth.

So who are we? We are divine sparks of Source, though various in the roles we play, there is an underlying canvas of consciousness that connects us. There really is nothing but Source, the Supreme Being. Here we were souls from various soul families that existed in other realms of creation. We came for an important transition for humanity, to evolve beyond human identities. We were here to demonstrate to humanity through our own evolution, removing the narrow boundaries created from human limitations. There are higher evolutionary virtues like compassion, cooperation, humility, service to others; and lower vibrational vices like fear, hatred, ignorance and arrogance. It was this differentiation between virtues and vices that man ignored and focused on the differences of identity like religion, nationality, gender and status.

Simply put, there are good and bad people in all religions and nationalities. It was also important for certain groups to move from exclusivity of 'heaven' for 'believers' to an inclusivity for all of humanity and beyond.

Our souls were given telepathic messages by our guides to keep nourishing our intuition and connection with our Inner Being as well as the Supreme Being. We were advised to live in the realm of energy, while adapting to the world of matter, to follow our inner guidance and trust our hearts. We were told that by our presence alone we would lift the vibration of earth and serve others by being an example. Lastly, our guides soaked us with a blissful light so loving and beyond comprehension. Rejuvenated, we were ready to return to our bodies that slept. That is how we spent our nights together, quite a contrast from what our characters were experiencing on the planet.

> *"Wrapped up in Yourself, You hid from me.*
> *All day I looked for You*
> *But when I found You hiding inside me,*
> *I ran wild, playing now me, now You."*

> — *Lal Deadh*

Chapter 3

The World that Came to Me

We left behind our chapter in Kashmir, along with all the family and friends we had there, and moved to India's capital, New Delhi. Abhi and I are six now. My father joined as a surgeon at a well-known hospital, and we shifted to a government provided bungalow. I got admission at the Convent of Jesus & Mary, a girls' Catholic school established by the British missionaries long ago, and my twin brother got into St. Columba's. Both schools were next to each other in the same complex and not too far from where we lived.

Central Delhi, where we lived, was green, open, clean, and quaint. Our house was on Park Lane, next to the large and beautiful Tālkatora Garden where we played, went on walks as a family, and stole mangoes to then be chased by the *Māli* (gardener).

One day, when we were seven, Abhi and I were hanging out with our neighborhood friend, Atul, after school. Standing with our bikes in our gravel driveway

Abhi, standing sternly, tensing his eyebrows, said in a bold voice, "Ok, I'm going to start a small neighborhood club".

He took out his notebook and dictated, "I will be the President. Atul you can be the Vice President".

Being left out and not understanding why, I asked, "What about me?"

"Eh! girls are not supposed to be leaders!" he said loudly, staring down at me, "you can follow as a member".

My heart felt crushed and I looked down sadly. Atul was meek and kinder, seeing me hurt, he convinced Abhi to make me Secretary. I kept quiet, still looking shaken, like a preyed upon victim. I wasn't satisfied with this consolation prize, feeling undervalued and more capable, but I had to suppress my feelings under the anger and control of my brother.

Abhi cycled off, "Come, let's go and get others to join," he said excitedly, and we followed on our bikes behind him.

The club didn't last long though, soon there were fights and quarrels, and no one was happy with the bullying of Abhi, so they quit and parted ways.

The cricket continued though; we went every evening to the open plot in our *mohalla* (sub-division) to play cricket. I was a tomboy and preferred to play sports with the boys rather than playing with dolls. Abhi had a big ego for his short, slim body. He was called 'out' by the umpire while batting during a cricket match.

With a warrior-like posture he stomped up close to the umpire, Sunil, and yelled at him face to face, "That's a no ball you fool!"

Timid little Sunil looked frozen with fright. My heart hurt, I ran to Sunil to console him and pulled him away from Abhi. Just another day in my life with Abhi.

It is funny that Abhi's anger and ego was like a paper tiger, because when it came to real danger, he buckled with fear, whereas I transformed into a lioness.

There was an Olympic size swimming pool near our house where we went swimming often. One day I decided to try diving from the diving board on the deep end. I started with the lowest board and managed to do so with much ease. So then I went to the middle diving board, and jumped into the pool, again without hesitation and with little difficulty went down and out of the water. I felt little to no fear to jump off the highest diving board, and as I climbed up the stairs to the board, the adults at the pool were astonished and told me to stop, some asked where my parents were, while Abhi ran towards home to call my dad. In the meantime, I just jumped into the pool with a surge of energy and excitement as I came down and landed in the pool. Abhi turned back to look aghast, jaw dropping, wide eyed. Then he walked up to the side of the pool to see me pop my head out of the water with a bright smile.

I climbed out of the pool and everyone was clapping, but Abhi was too proud to acknowledge and walked awkwardly away saying, "You're mad!"

The one who always showed me down to pamper his ego, could not follow my act here and chose to ignore it.

Abhi went running to tell my parents of my suicidal act, and they came running to the pool by which time I was being celebrated as a hero. My dad smiled proudly and came up to me, hugged me, then lifted me in his arms and started towards home. My mom joined us, scolding me and looking pale with fright, asking me if I was ok, and then asking me to promise I will never do it again. Abhi started a long winded commentary that he told me not to, a lie of course, and no one listened to him because it was my time to shine. Feeling neglected he slowed down his pace and followed us sulking.

As time went by Abhi and my differences became more pronounced, strange that we were twins, polar opposites and quite a contrast.

My mother was so loving, yet he felt unloved and jealous that my parents loved me more. Whereas I was so content with whatever I had and got, and so grateful for my parent's love. My mother was a good cook and even though our finances were scarce, we were always satisfied with good food. We used to come home from swimming, sit in front of the black and white TV, and Mummy used to give us milk and toast. The love of our life was the new addition to our family, a Russian Samoyed puppy, Rocky, whom we obsessed over him day and night. While there were stray dogs I saw suffering and broke my heart. I used to ask my mother why they were stray? Where did they find food? I didn't quite understand why no one did anything about them. More so was I tormented by the poor and the beggars I saw, it pained my heart deeply, so traumatic it was to see their plight. Abhi; however, seemed to be rather thick skinned and immune, or less sensitive than me.

My father played tennis quite well and used to take us for lessons in the evenings to Ganges Club near the President's mansion, *Rashtrapati Bhavan.* We took swimming lessons at Gymkhana Club on Sundays, followed by a garden buffet lunch. With its old English charm, Gymkhana club has always remained one of my favorite places in Delhi. Though my parents didn't have much of a bank balance, and my mother struggled to run the house, as children we enjoyed our innocence and had such a pristine childhood. Picnics with our maternal uncle and his family, board games in the cooler during summer, and many other simple family fun events etched beautiful memories in me forever. My father was adventurous, a mini James Bond, and loved to travel. My mother was extremely feminine and loved being home. Daddy had a good sense of humor, and his partner in crime, Bhushan uncle was even more hilarious and the best story teller we knew. So when they were together we rolled in laughter with stories and jokes.

We used to go to Kashmir in our summer holidays to stay with our uncle and aunt, in our family bungalow, and reunite with our old friends in Srinagar. Our paternal uncle and aunt were much more traditional than my open minded parents, and dominated over my parents being the patriarch which I never understood or liked. When I was younger I could never understand why Abhi was given special treatment by them, while I was ignored.

During the winter holidays we had fun at the Christmas parties at Gymkhana Club. On Christmas night our parents told us Santa would come at midnight, and we tried hard to stay awake to see him come. After we fell asleep, they used to keep gifts and stocking stuffers near our pillows, which we were so excited to see in the morning.

Often patterns that have occurred in past lives repeat in the current life. My parents were the same in a previous life in which my mother died from a complication in her pregnancy when I was around seven in that life. In this life a similar event occurred. My brother and I were in Srinagar with our aunt and uncle during the summer holidays, when we were called to Delhi urgently as my mother was critically ill. We were rushed there overnight and were taken straight to the hospital. We briefly saw my mother being taken from the ICU to the operating theater, with my father beside the gurney. She was in a semi-conscious state, but when my father told her that the children had come, she opened one eye slightly and looked deeply into my eyes, as though for the last time. I felt so confused and sad as I didn't know why my mother was so ill. She had an ectopic pregnancy, and her uterus had ruptured, fainting on the floor. Luckily my father was at home and was a doctor, so the ambulance arrived quickly. There was little chance of her surviving as she had lost most of her blood, however; the best surgeons in Delhi were in this hospital and they saved her miraculously. So in this life, with my soul's request and prayers, I didn't lose this source of unconditional love in my life, unlike the past life. In that life I suffered deep pain with the lack of unconditional love, and it scared my soul.

Satya Sai Baba was a famous spiritual master (Guru) of India. Once Satya Sai Baba had come to Talkatora Garden for an event. My mother took me with her to see him. I remember the masses of people, but nothing of what he said. I saw him sitting on the stage, leaving, coming back on stage, and starting blessing people with his hand gestures, but people started leaving and were oblivious to his presence. So I was confused. My mother held my hand to go.

"But" I said, "He's still there on stage. Why are people leaving?"

My mother was rather startled and thought I was mistaken. I wasn't, I could clearly see him there, and how come she couldn't? When I was older, I realized that it was Baba's astral form that I saw come back to the stage to bless people without their knowing. So it means that my, and perhaps many children's, third eye is open to see astral beings and the energetic realm.

As a teenager I was still ignorant about the world, and seemed to be in my own inner world, whereas Abhi knew so much about the outer world. He was smart, attracted to the sensual, and secretly did many dubious things which I had no clue about. I loved learning Indian history at school, and was drawn to temples and ancient texts. My uncle had booklets on the *Upanishads*, and a commentary on the *Bhagavad Gita*, which I used to secretly read. When he found out, I was given a lecture that I'm too young to read these books, and that these should be studied when older. I wondered why. Then there was Abhi who read magazines for adults with his *chelas* (friend followers).

One night when I was thirteen, I was on the terrace roof of our house (in India most homes have flat roofs that are like a terrace), I was pensive and looked out into the stars. I wondered if there was a state of mind without thoughts. My mind focused on one star without effort and I observed my thoughts till the last thought of 'I', which too disappeared. Then my mind seemed to go into a black hole. I ceased to see anything, all sound pulled into my ears, and I went into a void. I don't quite know how long I had blacked out. When Gonna Deadh came looking for me and held my arm, I came back to consciousness, though she said I had been gone for hours, I felt I had only blinked. Everyone was worried about where I was. My mind was still blank, though I was very alert and aware. The moon was behind us as we walked towards the stairs to go down, and suddenly we noticed that a bright light went around my shadow and my shadow disappeared. I was neither astounded nor scared, but Gonna Deadh screeched in shock and then looked at me with a strange face.

I was very peaceful, I smiled and said to her, "It's ok, I'm fine".

We stood there for a minute observing and then my shadow slowly came back. She then held my hand and rushed down the stairs with me, while I pleaded with her not to tell my parents. I went to my parents bedroom, while she covered her mouth with her Sari and went to the kitchen.

My parents were a bit annoyed and asked me where I had been, so I said, "on the roof, I just lost track of time".

I looked at the clock on the wall, the time was 11:11pm. We negotiated that I need to let someone know where I am before disappearing, and then I headed to bed.

That night I sat up and leaned back in bed because my energy was so high I couldn't sleep. My mind was still and wasn't running with thoughts like it usually did. Even though my eyes were open I was in meditation. I felt a gentle loving presence and smelled the fragrance of flowers, and though I couldn't see a physical form, I could 'see' subtle forms above me of Jesus and another master (whom I later found out was Sri Guru Babaji aka Maha Avatar Babaji). They were there to be with me that night, or perhaps it was them who bestowed that light onto me with their grace and blessings. From then on every night, I used to sit up in bed and meditate, on my own, without instruction or effort.

The flow of thoughts came from a higher mind, the innate ability to know things, as soon as I asked a question the answer would drop in my mind. I seemed to have other spiritual gifts like telepathy, seeing a person's subtle body, knowing their truth, their thoughts, and physical abilities like immense power to move large objects or throw a shot put a long distance. I was a track and field athlete and could run faster than anyone else to set a record for my school. All these superhuman abilities seemed natural to me, as though I always had them, and that they simply came back to me after a brief hiatus.

My new state of awareness continued from this point on in my life. It is a witness state of my own body, and of the world. Like when you are in a train, you can watch the world outside go by while you move ahead. There was a parallel life I led, one in which I was involved in the world, and another state where I observed myself transact in the world.

For me devotion was natural, whether it was a connection with Christ and his unconditional love, or the power of attraction towards Sri Krish, for whom I had a special place in my heart. It was as though Sri Krishn was always with me, and I had known him for eons. Krishn-ji was my constant companion, my role model, the only one who truly loved me, my Guru, and the only permanent support I had throughout my life.

———— ✦✦ ————

Abhi had a rather notorious high school. He had started drinking, smoking marijuana, and partying with the wrong crowd. My mother was intuitive and picked up that something was wrong, but my father being the eternal optimist dismissed her concerns. Problems with children never go away, they just change, in fact become more serious and complex. With every generation they seem to be happening earlier in age. Abhi's hormones brought libido full on. There was a family friend's daughter whom he liked and ended up having a relationship with. Though for Abhi it was more about having fun and not serious, it was on a deeper emotional level for her. They were just sixteen.

At eighteen Abhi and I went off to separate colleges. I was more inclined towards science and wanted to become a surgeon like my father, but my mother dissuaded me from living the life of a doctor. So I majored in Computer Science at a top engineering university in India. While Abhi wasn't sure what he wanted to do, and so he was counseled by my uncle to do economics at a local elite university. My rather calculative uncle and cunning aunt, who didn't have children, kept Abhi very close and invested in this relationship. My uncle hoped that Abhi would take over the family business from him.

I didn't want to go off to college in another city, as I was really apprehensive about the wild college life. I would rather stay at home and go to college locally. My mother believed in Satya Sai Baba, and she had a book on him which I was reading. In that book there was a black and white photo of Shirdi Sai Baba who lived in the early 20th century. When I looked at his photo, his eyes seemed to come alive and talk to me. I was fixated on it for a while. I told him, telepathically, I don't want to go to college away from home. A few months later we arrived at the train station with my bags packed to embark on the journey to college. My parents and the driver left the car to get a porter and tickets, while I sat in the back seat of the car. A short *Pandit* wearing clean ironed *kurta* and *dhoti*, well combed hair, a *Vaishnav tilak* on his forehead, and a *tulsi mala* around his neck, knocked on my car window. I rolled down the window a bit. He did *Namaste*, then started saying something in Hindi I couldn't initially register. I thought he was going to offer some religious service for money, so I wasn't paying attention.

"May your journey be happy and may you gain knowledge. May you prosper offering everything at the feet of the Lord. May your faith and devotion then be a shining example for humanity. Blessings of happiness, prosperity, and peace," saying these words he left.

I was quite puzzled who he was and why he came to talk to me. Strange. Was this the divine who came in form to bless me and give me a message before I began my journey alone to college?

College was a cultural change for me, and such a social shock. I was still too naive to mingle in the madness of the youth who found their freedom for the first time. Like attracts like and a few meek ones found good company in each other. I soon had a small set of close friends from all corners of India; Thomas a Keralite Christian boy, Bodhi a Buddhist Bihari young man, Shivaji a talented Maharashtrian male, Mina a Muslim girl from Bhopal (MP), and me a lost soul from Kashmir. Our group of five hung out most of the time to study together. We called ourselves '*The Elements*', for the five elements, ether, air, fire, water and earth. Engineering colleges in India are tough, we barely got time to do much else. Our university was in a very small town, there were no fancy restaurants there, nor could we afford them. Just outside the college premises there was a *Dhaba*, a roadside eatery, which students frequented. Our monthly pocket money was spent here over a simple rural meals and *chai*, especially after we finished our periodic exams. Though many, if not most, of the boys spent it on local liquor and pot sold undercover at the corner *Paan* stall. We developed close bonds, made many memories, and even in meager circumstances, found a way to have fun with the bare minimum. As we progressed to become Seniors, the pressure mounted and if it weren't for the supportive friendships, many would have broken down from the stress.

We have known the people we meet or have a relationship with in a previous life. There is a purpose in our interactions. Sometimes we feel a sense of familiarity when we meet someone for the first time, as though we have known them for a long time. Often we become close to someone very quickly, and feel a deep connection, or have a conflict that seems to be repeating a pattern that we are trying to learn how to resolve. Many of our meetings seem coincidental, but in fact they are destined, and planned. Most close relationships have been discussed and planned by souls before birth to work out some Karm. The five of us in college had known each other before. We were destined to meet in college to spend these formative years together to support and learn from each other. I started learning a lot about Islam and its practice from Mina, Buddhism from Bodhi, and Christianity from Thomas. It was like an immersive course in comparative religions.

Chapter 4

Bonding with the Divine

If there was one purpose I had for this life, it was to bond with the divine. Be one with that which is my very own nature, my Dharm, an innate nature of all things in creation. A mysterious self-guided force towards the Source is inborn in every soul. If at any time in my life I was not in alignment with the force flowing from the soul, I was not at ease. It meant I had lost that connection with my inner Self, and the Self was blocked from expressing itself through me. Therefore, there was an inner impetus to re-establish that pipeline between the Self and my personality. As anything that is dedicated to the Divine becomes pure, so I felt a deep conviction to dedicate my life to the Supreme. It was not to prove anything to anyone else, but it was my own inner journey.

I had several attractive job offers after completing my undergraduate in Computer Science. I chose one that was in Delhi, so that I could go back to living with my parents. Some of my friends went to Bangalore or Mumbai, and others abroad for their Masters. Mina also decided to take a job in Delhi where she could live with her aunt. Her family didn't allow her to go abroad unless she married someone there. In fact, they already had marriage proposals for her which she escaped for now. I was happy anyway; I had a college friend to hang out with in Delhi. So was she. We could disappear at night to have fun having Chaat at South Ex, or watch the latest Bollywood movie at Lajpat Nagar, or spend an enjoyable day at Connaught Place and Janpat.

I had a break of several months before I joined work, and my friends invited me to join them for a trip to Europe. But I wasn't interested. There was a two month Vedanta course at Sivananda Ashram, Divine Life Society, in Rishikesh which excited me.

"Come on! I did so well in college, I listen to everything you say, I just want to do this one thing I love," I begged my parents to allow me to go.

After much persuasion, I was elated when they said I could.

"Ok fine but you have to go with someone. Let's talk to your cousin, Gaurav, he loves to learn *Dharmic* things, I'm sure he'd love to go with you".

Gaurav was a staunch adherent to our family's spiritual tradition of Kashmiri Shaivism. He was more technique oriented as well as more disciplined than me. I was the opposite of traditional.

I was so excited and counting days till I left for Rishikesh. A pull so strong. My parents were afraid I might find a Guru at an ashram and never come back! Well, I was really interested in checking myself into a Himalayan cave, but perhaps I wouldn't quite fit the bill of an ascetic Sadhu.

"Well, well! our little Lalla is going to Rishikesh of all places for a break. Swami training," Abhi broke out into his typical disgusting satirical laugher.

"That's just so weird Lalla, for a girl your age, while your friends are going to Europe. I mean who goes to *Rishikesh*," Abhi grimaced, mocking me in his exaggerated theatrical style.

Somehow, I just ignored him, and didn't let his denigrating me crush my self-confidence or joy. I had a way to be in my own happy world. While in contrast, Abhi strived to maintain a self-image of being smart and successful. His general knowledge was impeccable, and I knew more about spirituality than many my age. We were mysterious twins, living in opposites. Complementary some might say.

⸻ ❖ ⸻

When we reached the beautiful foothills of the Himalayas, I felt I had come home. These mountains were full of the mystical experiences of so many over the ages.

As we crossed Lakshman Jhula, I looked around and reminisced the plethora of saints and sages that had attained enlightenment here and guided so many to attain *Moksh*. Even the air was filled with divine vibrations. I could not have had this opportunity by chance, things are destined and planned.

When I saw the 'Sivananda Ashram' painted above the entrance, I flew up the stairs in glee. My feet barely touching the ground. Like a magnet pulls steel, I felt drawn to this place. Gaurav was far behind, climbing up slowly. The ashram seemed so familiar, and I felt comfortable here immediately. I asked around for where we needed to register, got checked in and went to our rooms. I was assigned a double room with another female participant, and Gaurav likewise. After washing up, we went down to the hall where everyone had assembled. A young Sadhu was talking to the participants saying that we will first go to attend the Ganga Aarti at sunset, followed by dinner, after which we will have a short orientation.

The Ganga Aarti was held on the banks of the Ganga at Parmarth Niketan Ashram which was right across the river. Only a fifteen-minute walk over the Ram Jhula (bridge).

When I first reached the banks of the Ganga, it seemed so vibrant, flowing with such energy. I felt so thrilled, a shiver went up my spine. The Ganga felt sacred, a sentient Being. In fact everything here did, nothing was inert, the whole place was alive, reverberating with a presence one could sense. Using my breath, I attuned my vibrations to the higher vibrations present here, like one tunes an instrument to a musical scale.

There were many Sadhus and Swamis, Gurus and Pundits assembled for the Ganga Aarti, all draped in shades of orange.

The row of priests, the Pujaris, climbed onto their individual daisies facing the Ganga and everyone fell silent. The ceremony proceeded with chants and chimes of various instruments and culminating in the priests circulating a giant lamp lit with many wicks, followed by another huge lamp burning camphor. This along with the ringing of bells and blowing of conches really lifted everyone's spirits.

After dinner and orientation, we went to our rooms. I was exhausted after a long day. I met my roommate, Uma Shankaran, who introduced herself. She was wearing a white sari with a deep red border, draped very neatly. She was holding her night clothes on her way to the washroom. I; however, was dressed casually in my kurti and pants, probably looking like a rookie.

"Is this your first time here?" she asked me in a serious voice.

"Yah...how about you?" I replied coolly.

She seemed confident and comfortable here.

"Oh…I come here every year," she said, pushing up her eyeglasses. "I'm associated with Chinmaya Mission Kerala. Our Guru, Swami Chinmayananda, began his spiritual journey here at this ashram with Swami Sivananda ", she explained.

"Oh yes! I've got a copy of Swami Chinmayananda's commentary on the Bhagavad Gita," I responded happily.

She nodded and smiled and proceeded to the washroom. Lights out and I crashed exhausted.

At 5am sharp we were to be present for yoga. After a quick bucket bath, I ran down the stairs to the platform deck next to the Ganges where we did yoga & meditation. When I opened my eyes slightly, there was the sun, its gentle hues rising above the horizon. I chanted the *Gayatri* mantra in my mind. The teacher started chanting some morning mantras and we followed along. Many adherents were on the banks of the Ganga, chanting, offering water to the sun, taking a dip in the Ganga, and doing the Sandhya Vandanam (the ancient morning/evening prayer to purify oneself through mantras). What a beautiful sight. If only the rest of the world was so peaceful.

Food at ashrams is generally simple and *Sattvic* (pure). We had breakfast and a break before we went to the main hall where our first knowledge session would begin.

Gaurav and I sat next to each other in great anticipation. The senior most Swamiji, Swami Chidananda, entered the hall dressed in an orange robe, and we all got up to offer our *Pranams* (a reverential salutation). Swamiji was boney, slim, and simple. He had a glow on his face and an energetic presence. After he sat on stage cross legged, we all got seated. I could sense the reverence everyone had for Swamiji, as is the tradition in this ancient culture of knowledge. Swamiji closed his eyes, folded his hands in prayer, invoked the presence of the Guru and started chanting the Shanti mantras. This is to prepare and purify the space to receive knowledge.

Everyone's mind seemed silent and peaceful as Swamiji started.

"Today we will start our journey into 'Kashmir Shaivism in the light of Vedanta'. Which is not a common topic. We will explore the similarities and differences between these two ancient schools of thought".

Gaurav turned to me smiling in glee and shifted in his seat with eagerness. He was keen on the theoretical aspects of Kashmiri Shaivism. I was here to learn, to experience knowledge as an awakening, to integrate into my life, not just for intellectual gymnastics. Any adventures to mystical places while I was here would be a bonus.

Swamiji first covered the etymology and meaning of Vedanta and Kashmiri Shaivism. Of course, he mentioned the works of Abhinavagupta, after whom my twin brother was named.

"Our contemporary, Swami Lakshman Joo, a master of Kashmiri Shaivism, has also spoken on a comparison of Vedanta and Kashmir Shaivism, and so has Swami Sivananda," said Swamiji.

He gave a summary to start, "The foundation of both schools of thought are based on the principle of Advaita, which is the ultimate Oneness within which all realities exist. The descent of that One Cosmic Consciousness is also explained in similar ways. Creation being a reflection of that One Consciousness, like a dream, is also explained in a similar way in both traditions. This is a summary of what we will explore in more depth in the sessions that follow. If we can look past the labels and terms used by these two traditions, and focus on the essence being conveyed, we will find more similarities than differences".

After a short pause and some reflection Swamiji continued, "If Truth is one, why, you may ask, should there be differences in explaining the Truth between those who have attained the Truth? Their definitions of Truth, that is Sat, and of Moksh or enlightenment may not be the same, and even the terms used by various masters can vary. This can be very confusing to truth seekers. So which explanation of Truth is correct? And which school of thought, path and practice should one choose?

Though Truth is one, its expressions and experiences are infinite.

In our inclusive Vedic tradition, all paths to Truth are honored, and they add to the wealth of wisdom available to truth seekers. As is in a university, with many schools, subjects, and professors. A student can choose a path they feel the most affinity with, the one which resonates with their nature, and most importantly is the path that is most appropriate for their stage of soul evolution".

With these enlightening and soul-searching words, Swamiji concluded the morning session.

There were about two hundred odd participants in the course. We started mingling with each other over lunch and hearing each others' stories. The table on which Gaurav and I were sitting had a couple of other young aspirants who were talking about going to Mouni Baba's cave. This cave had so many mystical tales associated with it. We were excited to join them. We were like a bunch of high school students on a camping trip.

Mouni Baba's cave was about an hour's walk, and we had to rush to be back for the 3 o'clock session. We crossed over the Ganges and passed many temples of all types, many ashrams of various Guru lineages, Yoga centers, and many people were busy in various spiritual activities. Then we left the small shops and roadside eateries behind and went into a wooded area in a hilly terrain. The path we took was the Nilkanth Mountain trek, and we stopped briefly at the beautiful Nilkanth falls where people were bathing. We proceeded quickly to the spot where there was a sign on the road which pointed towards a narrow pathway to Mouni Baba's cave.

The rugged path led down along the hillside to a cemented platform which had a Shiv ling, and a stand above it was a pot dripping water on the Shivling. No one else was here except us. As we walked around the platform, we saw an opening on the side of the hill, which seemed to be an entrance into the cave, so we walked in. It was a reasonably small cave that could fit a few people, the ceiling was low, so we crouched as we went further in. Over the years some people had put some tiles and cement in places to hold the structure perhaps. There were paintings on the walls of Shiva, Gurus and Swamis we didn't recognize. At the end of the cave, was a small niche where there was a statue of a Yogi sitting cross legged, and under that on a plaque was written, 'Shri Guru Babaji - also known as Maha Avatar Babaji'. There was a tiny altar under the statue with Puja offerings, a Shiva's trident, a Kalash (tumbler) with water, and other articles. It seemed as though this cave was being maintained and visited often by people. As I turned around, I saw Gaurav had already sat down, cross legged, and started meditating. The three of us got the cue from him and sat down to meditate as well. That is when we truly felt the cave, in that stillness there was so much life. As though the cave was talking to us, transmitting the vibrations of eons of holy sages that had meditated here. The top of my head was tingling, and I either fell asleep or went into a void.

The next thing I heard was Gaurav saying, "Let's go. It's time to go, we must not be late".

I opened my eyes, still in stillness, and brought myself back into the present moment quickly. Apparently twenty minutes had passed, and I didn't realize it. I felt fresh and recharged. I got up without feeling tired anymore. I folded my hands, bowed down to Babaji, touching my forehead to the floor. Then we left the cave and quickened our pace down the path back to our ashram to join our next knowledge session.

❋

After dinner we sat for a bit with a group of our newly acquired friends on the platform deck overlooking the Ganga. The river looked so serene, with the moonlight reflecting sparkles on its waves. The crickets were chirping, and a cool moist breeze made the atmosphere very pleasant. One person in the group, Aditya, was telling us a story about how an astral form of Shivananda appears often in the meditation room in the wee hours of the morning. Some Swamis and disciples who have meditated in the meditation hall between 3 and 4am have seen his form that appears in a light form. Some folks got spooked and left for their rooms. Rest of us were hooked on hearing more mystical stories, especially firsthand experiences, but soon we retired for the night for an early start the next morning.

We absorbed ourselves in the knowledge sessions, and often discussed the topics afterwards. It was also a lot of fun interacting with participants, pulling each other's leg, and enjoying our small excursions to ancient spiritual spots that we had only read about in books.

One weekend some of us decided to hire a taxi and go up to Rudraprayag, a few hours' drive from Rishikesh. Located at the confluence (Prayag) of the roaring Alaknanda and Mandakini rivers, it is an amazing site to see. With immense mountains in the backdrop, white water gushing through their lap, a V shaped crag between the two rivers as they meet, and a temple perched there at the tip. Several other buildings of ashrams and resting places are dotted here and there. There were many pilgrims visiting this holy site, as well as several ascetics, the Sadhus and Aghori Babas - they are well known in these regions. Aghoris generally reside in remote places away from people, like caves or temples where they do long periods of intense spiritual practices, and are distinctly recognized by their ash smeared bodies, matted hair, holding tridents or a long walking stick. Who knows how many ascetic Yogis were in deep long meditative states somewhere up in the Himalayan caves, we have only heard stories that they exist. Even in the freezing cold winters in the snow, these yogis can be scantily clad and barely eat, as they are able to generate internal heat and energy from their Sadhana (spiritual practices including Pranayama, Yoga postures and Dhyan).

We rested here at Rudraprayag for lunch, and walked down the steps from the temple to the rocky riverbed. The roar of the rivers and mist filled the air, with temple bells ringing faintly in the background. It is an unimaginable feeling, not just for the natural beauty, but the divinity of it. From ancient times, great Rishis, enlightened beings, have walked this sacred land, to absorb in the vibrations of their investment, is truly a blessing.

We spent the night in Rudraprayag, and next day on our way back to Rishikesh, we stopped at Devprayag, the meeting of Alaknanda and Bhagirathi, and both rivers thereafter flow on as the river Ganga. Therefore, it is the birthplace of the Ganges. Devprayag was a slightly bigger town with several buildings and temple complexes. We were sitting on the steps outside the temple which led down to the river. The morning Puja had ended, and people were walking out of the temple.

There was a Swamiji dressed in orange with a small group of people bowing to him and asking him some questions. We got up and did Pranams to be respectful. He turned and looked at us and asked us where we had come from. Some of us responded to him, and I said I came to Rishikesh for a summer course.

Suddenly, he started talking to me as though he knew me, "Don't worry no matter what you do for a living, you will always stay connected to the Supreme. You'd rather follow a spiritual life than work or get married, am I right?"

I was quite stunned, my jaw dropping, so I stumbled some words out of my mouth nodding, "Umm...yeah... yes".

He continued with a smile, "You are a devotee of Sri Krishn born in a Kashmiri Shaivite family. Do not feel that a worldly family life is opposed to a spiritual life. In this life you will integrate both".

Still quite shocked at his words, I just folded my hands and touched his feet, then he blessed me and moved on.

I was still absorbing his words, standing still, when Gaurav and my friends huddled around me whispering in exhilaration, "What was he saying!" and "How did he know?" etc.

One friend asked someone nearby who he was. We were told his name is Swami Siddhananda who had an ashram in the holy city of Haridwar.

Well, that was an experience to remember and a story to share. At least we got to meet one of the many evolved souls present in these areas. Bharat has had and still has innumerable Gurus, and Siddhis are commonplace, not that spiritual abilities are necessary or a sign of evolution, they are a natural outcome as the soul ascends.

At each critical juncture in my life some divine guidance always came through someone, like this Swamiji who reassured me about integrating the inner and outer worlds. Towards the end of our two-month sojourn in Rishikesh, I hoped we had done justice to this sacred land. Though I felt something was missing, perhaps I had a deep desire to have spent my time here with a true Guru, who would have guided me in the way of the ancient Guru-disciple tradition. Like the way Balakrishna Menon had found Tapovan Maharaj, who later became Swami Chinmayananda, and many other such stories. Was this tradition becoming extinct? Or would I ever find my Guru?

It was hard leaving Rishikesh and all the friends we had made. We promised to stay in touch and have a reunion the following year. As we tore ourselves away from the near perfect environment of Rishikesh, and descended down the hills towards Delhi, it seemed as though we exited a bubble of higher vibrations and were back to the land of Maya. Still charged with the pure energies of the holy Himalayas, our faces glowed, we were told, when we returned home.

Chapter 5

Stepping into the World

Abhi was getting ready to go to London for his MBA when we returned. Everyone was busy with getting things ready for his departure. Relatives and friends also came to meet him before he left. Our paternal uncle, Petar, was sponsoring his education, investing in him, as our humble parents could not afford to do so. It took me a few days to adjust the hustle and bustle of Delhi and activity at home. The only personal time I got to ponder and meditate was in bed. The house seemed so quiet once Abhi departed, as he soaked up most of the attention.

I had to quickly shift gears to get ready for my first day at work, from spirituality to science, from the inner to the outer world. My mother was a Shirdi Sai Baba devotee and took me to a local Sai temple to get blessings for an auspicious start. I was a bit nervous and felt a little awkward on my first day in formal clothes in an office. I toiled through my first week, commuting, sitting at a desk all day, and the formal work environment. I was so relieved when the weekend arrived. Over the first few weeks I made some friends who were also new and those in my team. My manager was very formal and serious. It doesn't cost to smile, right? I didn't feel comfortable asking him questions so I was lucky that a team member became a mentor. Days seemed so long and tiring, the tension caused migraines in me. Just a sign that a work life was not really my cup of tea. Regardless, I did my work with dedication and commitment. The work was interesting, and I was learning a lot. Programming and logic came to me naturally, so did conceptual design. Problem solving was fun, and technology exciting. Before I knew it, months had passed, and I became used to the routine of going to work.

One night in a week I went to Chinmaya Mission Delhi for talks on Gita or Upanishads. It was nice to have a Satsang there with other aspirants. There were many other spiritual centers in Delhi, like Rama Krishna Mission that I used to visit. I also loved going to temples with my family. I had a group of spiritual friends that made plans to go to these places and also attend local workshops and retreats. Some of my friends were also learning Rekhi, energy healing, and others were learning TM (Transcendental Meditation) from Maharishi Mahesh Yogi.

In the background my parents had started looking for a match for me. My mother had asked me my thoughts on marriage, and deep inside I knew that in this life I had to lead a worldly life, so I agreed to get married. She was so relieved as earlier I had told her I didn't want to marry, adamant that I wanted to live in an ashram. This had got her very worried. I didn't want to be the cause of any sadness for my parents either, which was another reason I decided to be a good girl. There was no doubt in my mind that my parents loved me dearly and wanted the best for me.

As is typical in many Indian families, there's always an aunt or someone who's a good match maker. So in ours, one of my paternal aunts, Girija Poff, was a natural go-between. She used to frequent weddings, eye potential candidates and discuss the prospects with their parents. In her purse she used to keep photos of young men and women, quickly taking one out when proposing a partner for someone's child. She lived in Srinagar during summer, and Delhi in winters. She came visiting one day, and my mother served tea and snacks. Sipping from her cup she asked my parents what they had thought about my marriage. My mother responded that they were eager to find a suitable match for me (before I changed my mind).

There was a young Kashmiri Pandit boy in the US who was doing his residency in neurosurgery from Stanford, she said, and would start working as a surgeon in two years. My aunt pulled out his photo and bio from her purse. His name was Siddharth Kashyap, he was five years older than me, fair, slim, and tall. He came from a prominent family of India, and his extended family details were also discussed. Family background is very important when selecting a bride or groom. In Indian culture it was a coming together of two families, not just individuals. Also, a cultured family meant that the children were brought up with good values and etiquette. My parents liked what they heard and thought that he would be a good partner for me.

At night my mom came to my room when I was getting ready for bed and approached the topic delicately. She started describing a young man who's very educated in the field of science, and is known to be gentle and mature. I listened quietly while looking for my night clothes, knowing my mother was being careful so that I wouldn't react with an immediate 'No'. She suggested that we meet him once, as he was coming to India soon, and then we can take it from there. She showed me his photo as I was hanging my clothes, I looked at it from the corner of my eyes. I didn't really have any feelings one way or another and told my mother that I would go along with whatever they thought was best. There was a condition though, I told her, that I will take my time to get to know him, and it may take several months, and he can also do the same. Then we can decide whether we're compatible and suitable for marriage. My mother agreed hesitatingly. It was not customary in those days for girls and boys to spend a lot of time together before a wedding, let alone have a relationship. Any breakup after a courtship usually brought a lot of embarrassment or dishonor for the family, which also made it difficult to find another match, especially for a girl.

My aunt connected the parents to exchange information and converse. Siddharth's mother also worked with their family *Brahmin* (priest), to see if his and my Vedic birth charts indicated if we were compatible in various areas. That test passed, and then his parent's planned to come visit after Siddharth arrived.

Siddharth and I met for the first time in October at our house, where we hosted him and his family for high tea. My paternal uncle and aunt (*Petar* and *Pechen*) also joined. I was dressed in a simple but elegant *Churidar*. They had arrived and were being seated and served in the living room first before my mother called me to join. I was feeling awkward and shy entering into such a setup situation, but the elders tried their best to make it natural and comfortable. I'm sure I was blushing. I did my *Namaste* and hello, barely making eye contact with Siddharth. He had a bright, peaceful face and a graceful presence. The parents were doing most of the talking till his mother asked me a question, and we got into a conversation. Siddharth's older brother, who apparently was already married, had also come, as well as his younger sister. I felt more comfortable talking to his sister, Aarti, as she was bubbly and friendly. Siddharth's mother,

Neelu aunty, was admiring our garden, as my parents were expert gardeners, so my parents decided to give them a tour.

While out in the garden the parents went ahead as a group discussing plants and flowers, while Aarti, Siddharth, his brother Akhil, and I staggered behind. Sid was talk and slender and had a graceful gait. His brother Akhil seemed lost in his thoughts and was looking around. Aarti looked inquisitively at both Sid and me, listening to our conversation attentively with a bright smile. We were talking about our colleges and common connections, as well as our current careers.

Siddharth asked me softly, smiling, "What are you doing right now? I mean where do you work? By the way, you can call me Sid".

I explained in reply and asked him the same. His answer seemed very intellectual and thorough, yet he made sure he communicated and connected. I could gauge his deep thinking, scientific bent of mind, and also his heart-based approach. It was much easier from then on to talk to him as he was kind enough to make me feel comfortable.

Such was our first meeting and we met once more before he returned to America. The second time, Aarti, him and I met in Connaught Place to have lunch and hang out. It was a lot of fun. This time we were more relaxed as the parents were not around and we could be more casual. We kept in touch over phone calls and letters, and their frequency increased over the next few months. There were many things we had in common, but most of all we gave each other equal respect. In contrast to Abhi who mocked my spiritual side, Sid surprisingly took genuine interest in my spiritual life and asked me deeper questions. He was quite accomplished himself, but I didn't sense a big ego in him. Sid seemed to live a healthy and purposeful life without any bad habits, as I would not get along with a smoker or drinker. At the moment he was focused on establishing himself in his new position as a doctor, and spent long hours studying. He also found time to write poetry, do photography, try new recipes, as well as researching and writing on different topics. He said he wanted to become a neurosurgeon and was applying for Fellowship positions. Even though he was not spiritual, he was knowledgeable about our Kashmiri Shaivism tradition and was keen on learning more. At least for now he accepted and praised my spiritual side, and said he believes in giving space and support for each other's paths. I soon realized he was quite mature for his age, and wise in his own way, kudos to his upbringing as well.

Sid seemed keen to come and meet me again after six months. Even though he wasn't very expressive about his feelings, and balanced them wisely, I knew he was interested in furthering our relationship, and I didn't mind. I wanted to go slow, as I knew the first stage of courtship is the honeymoon period, where the other person seems so attractive and perfect. Slowly, the spots, dents and negative patterns appear. This could further escalate to conflict and breakup, or a turn for the better towards resolution and love. So, I wanted to go full cycle to see both the positive and negative sides, and see if our relationship survived this test, then perhaps we were compatible.

Our parents were observing us very closely and inquisitive about our interactions. My mother came to know that he is coming to visit, and suggested that if I liked him, we should get engaged. I reminded my mom what she had once told me, that it takes about a year to know someone, and not to rush into any relationship without discernment. So I wanted to be careful as it was a question about my life and future family. She backed down as she sensed I was quite firm and didn't want a confrontation. It was harder for my more conservative *Petar* and *Pechen* to understand how a boy and girl can meet and engage without any commitment for marriage. They were more liberal with my brother though, he could get away with having a girlfriend in London.

It was nice to see Sid again. His parent's called us for dinner, and he was waiting outside to receive us. There was a lot more casualness and laughter this time around, as we got a bit more comfortable with each other, though keeping up our guards. Aarti, Sid and I got to talk more after dinner as we toured his home, Aarti pulling her brother's leg, giggling, on how he is waiting eagerly to meet me. Made both of us embarrassed. I was still thinking about our interactions on our drive back home, and as I went to bed.

We had long conversations on the phone and met a few more times, but never alone. It was always exhilarating meeting and spending time with him. I got more time to open up and talk about my career and spiritual side. He was surprisingly open, accepting and supportive. For me, respect for a wife by a husband was more important than love. Love is often conditional.

Sid approached the topic of getting engaged indirectly, suggesting his parents were keen on moving forward and liked me very much. It felt like I was having a Deja vu, as though I was observing the scene from outside my body. I couldn't speak, and barely responded. This was followed by his parents calling mine expressing their desire to have the children engaged before Sid left.

I prayed to Sai Baba and Krishn for guidance and grace that night, as I did every night. At night I used to meditate in bed, or read and ponder. Sometimes I looked at Sai Baba's photo and talked to him. I told him that I don't want to go to America, I want to stay in Bharat, the land of the Vedas, and also close to my parents. I also asked Baba, Krishn, and the Supreme, if Sid was the right person for me. If I married Sid, it meant I would have to move to the US.

I looked at Sai's photo in the book my mom had given me one night, and conversed with him mentally again saying,

'*Baba I don't want to leave my parents, I don't like America, I don't want to go there*'.

I heard a soft subtle male voice within me say, '*You have known him before…you have been together before. It is meant to be*'.

Feeling peaceful and relieved I slipped into sleep.

The next morning when my mother sat down for puja, I approached and told her that I was ok with getting engaged. Even though I was initially hesitant, I was agreeing as I knew it would be difficult to prolong an non-committal relationship any longer. My mother kissed me and said that she also felt in her heart that this boy is the right one for me.

We had a beautiful, simple and joyous engagement, *Gandun*, ceremony in our home, with all family members, neighbors, and close friends. In Indian culture each relationship has a unique name, not just generic cousin, uncle, aunt, etc. *Maam, Mamin* (mother's brother and wife) and their two children (cousins I was close to), *Maasi* (mother's sister), and her son, *Poff, Poffu* (father's sister and husband), and of course *Petar, Pechen*, were all present. Abhi couldn't come as it was short notice. Sid, his family, some extended family members, and some close friends came over. Our '*Kul Brahmin*' (priest), Prakash Boi, and Girija Poff, who was an expert at the Kashmiri customs, conducted the ceremonial part called

Kasamdry. As part of every ritual in Kashmiri Pandits an elderly lady of the family does some cleansing of any bad vibes (called *Nazar* in other cultures) that may affect a person, and she will do it for the main people in the ceremony. First some embers are burnt in a clay pot held in a wicker basket, called *Kanger*, she then takes out some *Isband* (Peganum harmala) seeds from a cloth handbag in her hand and touches the forehead and both shoulders, then tosses these seeds onto the embers to take away and burn any bad vibes. In our case my eldest *Poff* performed this energy/aura cleansing for Sid, me, and our parents. Then we had the ring exchange. We were blessed by all the elders, showered with flowers, coins, toffees, and almonds by the elders. It felt divine. It was so fulfilling to see my parents happy and celebrating. This was followed by a grand Kashmiri feast. Sid seemed over the moon. I had mixed feelings though, and my mind was a bit blank. It was hard to digest that I just got engaged!

Prakash Boi sat down with both parents separately in another room after the luncheon to find a suitable wedding date, called *Muhurat,* as per the Vedic astrology (*Jyotish*). The rest of us continued the celebration with lots of jest, laughter, and conversations over Kashmiri tea. Our parents emerged from the room and announced the wedding will be in about six months, on April 14th. Everyone cheered with elation. Sid looked at me deeply and smiled. I felt shy and nervous. My mother came and hugged me, kissing me on my cheeks. Then dad came and hugged and blessed me. They also congratulated Sid. Sid's parents came over as well, his mom placed a kiss on my forehead. There is a lot of hugging and kissing on the foreheads in Kashmiri Pandits. Usually it's male to male, and female to female.

Soon after they left everyone in our family felt so happy and relieved that everything went well.

Sid left for America in a couple of days. Wedding preparations started immediately. My parents, uncle and aunt also traveled to several cities to buy things from places that specialize in those items. The wedding was going to be in Srinagar, so we made trips there to plan and prepare. I wanted a traditional wedding at our ancestral home, where my uncle and aunt lived. Time went by very quickly and it was already April. Our Haveli was thoroughly cleaned. Our amazing family cook (*waza*) and his son, who had many of our family weddings under his belt, prepared a temporary outside kitchen, with a big mud and brick stove (*wur*), where mouthwatering Kashmiri vegetarian dishes were cooked over the next week or so. There was an army of additional house help that were added as well.

Everyone started arriving a week before the wedding, including Abhi. We had booked a hotel for Sid's guests, while Sid's family stayed at their ancestral bungalow. My close friends from college, Mina, Thomas, Shivaji, and Bodhi, all came, as well as some friends from high school. My local childhood friends in Srinagar also joined in. Our immediate relatives stayed at our house, and other family members at our neighbors and friends' homes, and a guest house was arranged. At least a hundred extended family members and friends had come from our side alone, plus there would be neighbors and local people as well. The wedding would have around three to four hundred guests. The house was beautifully decorated like a bride with flowers and festival lights. Sid's family and mine had separate functions in our own homes over five days. Elderly ladies dressed in fine *pherans* and *taranga* (headscrafts), sang *wanvun* (Vedic wedding *slokas* sung in chorus) on *tumbaknaer* (hand drum), harmonium, and other instruments every day after dinner, as is the tradition.

Our Haveli was full of music, laughter and festivity. Nephews, nieces that I met for the first time, great aunts I hadn't met since childhood. So many cousins and extended family members all made it a grand family event. I was the center of attraction which I wasn't used to. Everyone was having fun in their own groups, like I was with my close friends and cousin sisters, Abhi hung out with cousin brothers and his friends.

In one of the ceremonies, *maenziraat,* my Poff, washed my hands and feet. This was followed by the

Mehndi (henna) ceremony, which started with my *Poffs*, putting henna on my hands and feet symbolically as a sign of auspiciousness.

Another ceremony was done where I (and Sid in his home) wore white linen clothes and my family members poured a little milk mixed with rose petals over me, to give me a purifying bath.

The day before the wedding ceremony, Sid, his family members and a Brahmin (priest) went to a Shiv temple to pray and seek blessings. On my side, all the ladies and I went to a Devi temple, and then did a Puja at home as well. This is called *Devagon* in the Kashmiri tradition, and is an ancient tradition for all Hindus. Even in the *Ramayan*, Sita ji went to a Devi temple the day before her wedding ceremony.

Wedding day arrived; everyone was running around getting things done. Ladies getting ready together, rushing to the salon and back. In the evening the boy's family and guests started their celebratory procession (*Baraat*) with music and dance towards our house. The whole house was dressed beautifully like a bride. As they arrived at our gate, Sid, the broom's male family members and guests were garlanded by my male family members. A decorated circle like a mandala had been made, two small plates with fruit, flowers and sweets were kept on this for the bride and groom. Sid came and stood on one side of this circle while the ladies sang Kashmiri wedding songs. I proceeded from the house in my red bridal sari and traditional jewelry, especially a gold ornament tied around my head. My *Poffs'* sons accompanied me holding the four corners of a decorated cloth canopy over me. I joined Sid and stood on his left side on the circle. One of my aunts first circulated a small pot of water on a plate around our heads. Another aunt then did the *Kanger* ritual. My mother then approached us with a plate of Indian dessert, picked up one piece and offered it to Sid to take a small bite, then to me to have a small bite, and alternated a couple of times. One of our other aunts then showered us with flower petals, almonds, candy and coins.

Everyone then proceeded towards the garden which was covered by a huge canopy where guests were gathered. There was a stage beautifully decorated with two ornate armchairs on it for the bride and groom. Sid and his immediate family stepped onto the stage. My parents helped me up the steps onto the stage. We were then asked to sit on the armchairs, and the guests came up one by one to wish us. After a long photo op with all the friends and family members, dinner was laid. The boy's family and their guests were seated and served by my family members.

Much after dinner was over, and most of the guests left, with a smaller number of close friends and family, the actual wedding fire ritual (*havan*) started which also involved parents and other family members' participation. Sid and I took the *pheras*, rounds around the sacred fire, seven times, for the seven vows as husband and wife. This is the main part of the Hindu wedding ceremony. At the culmination, both of us were covered with a red shawl and showered with flowers, coins, candy, and almonds by everyone. This is called *Posh Puza*, and is a very important part of Kashmiri weddings. My uncle and aunt blew a conch to commemorate an auspicious beginning to married life.

By the time the wedding ended it was late night. It was time for me to officially depart with Sid and my in-law's home (*waerev*). My family members gave their respects and bid farewell to Sid's family. Lots of gifts were given and sent separately to Sid's entire family. My parent's also ordered many household things for Sid and me to start our life together. It is a very emotional moment, as it's a big milestone in life to step away from your parents into your in-law's family. My mother was crying letting her daughter go away from her, and I hugged my parents tightly, whispering I'll be back the next day to comfort them. Abhi put his arm around my shoulders and led me to a flower decked car and helped me in. My younger cousin was going to come with me to my in-laws this first night, as is the tradition, and he sat in the front seat. Sid got into the car next to me. He looked at me concerned and handed me his handkerchief, as I looked down with tears running down my cheeks and emotions hard to handle. It was very difficult leaving my parents behind and moving forward with a relatively unknown family. Everyone was somber. Both the families exchanged pleasantries, and our entourage left for Sid's family home in Srinagar.

The next day, Abhi came to pick me up and I did come back to my parent's home, along with my cousin who had come with me. Even though I came for a few hours it was a big relief, and that's why this tradition is there, to comfort a young bride who goes to her new home for the first time. Now things have changed a lot and women are older when they get married, and come back often to their parents. I picked up all my things from home and I was dropped off at the airport by my parents and Abhi. I joined Sid and his family at the airport and we departed for Sid's parent's home in Delhi.

Chapter 6

A Budding Married Life

I arrived at Sid's family home with the groom's party, where several ceremonies and events followed. There was a grand dinner reception with many distinguished guests. My immediate family and some extended family members were also present. Sid's father was a humble nobleman from a well-known Kashmiri Pandit family. He was retired now from his top administrative position, so many government officials and politicians were also present at the reception. My mother-in-law was very graceful and kind, she made me feel comfortable and calm. Sid's sister Aarti and I were good friends now, so she was a good companion for me. Sid's older brother, Akhil, and his wife, Priya, were warm and protective. Priya helped me a lot with understanding Sid's family traditions and adapting to my new family. I found his family very cultured and refined. Sid always kept an eye on me and made sure I was comfortable and happy. He was very supportive in my engagement with his family and stayed by my side while mingling with a plethora of relatives and guests in the first week after our wedding.

We went off for our honeymoon to Sikkim and had a wonderful break after the whirlwind of wedding activities. Once we were back, Abhi came over to escort me to my parent's home in Delhi. It is traditional for brides to go back after being with her in-laws for a few days, which is a very comforting break. Abhi looked subdued, very unlike his usual arrogant angry image. He seemed rather quiet during our ride home, and immediately went to his room once we arrived. My mother was eagerly waiting for me at the door and was so happy to see me. I could finally change into my casuals and take off my Sari and jewelry, uffh! Felt so relieved. Oh, it was so good to be home.

After my mom sent Abhi to run some errands, my parents shared the saga of Abhi's intense breakup with his girlfriend in London. There was a lot of emotional upheaval and anxiety that Abhi went through which my parents also got pulled into. At one point he even became suicidal, was depressed, and almost quit his MBA program, I was told.

All this was kept from me of course, and Abhi didn't share this even with our parents until after my wedding. My mother's homeopathic medicines helped settle him a bit now. My poor parents, I thought. It was so tiring taking care of my wedding, with no rest, to now be drained emotionally with my brother's breakup woes. While my father was less emotional and more pragmatic, my mother was very worried and anxious. Mummy's solution was, of course, to find him a good Kashmiri girl and get him married, while Daddy wanted to straighten him out and get him to be more sensible. Hearing this complicated melodrama that transpired between Abhi and his girlfriend, I felt that Abhi got too involved too quickly without giving time to the relationship to see the true nature of his partner. Just then Abhi walked through the front door, and we abruptly ended our conversation. Abhi looked at us and realized we had probably been talking about him.

I was too scared to breach the topic with him, not knowing how he would react. In the evening I asked Abhi to come with me to my favorite Chinese restaurant in Vasant Vihar. I distracted him with music and conversations about Sid and my in-laws, hoping that it would take the attention away from himself. He didn't retract with his usual sarcasm and demeaning verbiage. I was surprised, and wondered what had mellowed him. After dinner we went to a Paan shop, we sat in the car and talked. I asked him about his studies and if he would like to come to the US to find a job, as Sid and I would be there. He sighed and looked away.

Then he began opening up and sharing, "I don't know Lalla. I have no idea where I am headed in my life. Everything seems to have fallen apart. I feel I have no future. I know I'm distressing Mom-Dad, but they don't understand what I'm going through".

He assumed our parents had briefed me about the situation, so he didn't go into the details. Initially I was really taken aback and pleasantly surprised with his sharing so authentically with me. He would never make himself vulnerable to me or anyone in the past.

After a long pause, I said softly, "Give yourself some time Abhi, after a month or so, you will feel much better. I think you should spend time with people who love you and inspire you. Maybe take a break and go on a trip, like a hiking trip in Kashmir or Himachal. You'll enjoy that, it will refresh your mind and settle your emotions. You know that I'm always there for you".

"Yah, I know Lalla," he said, "when are you guys leaving for California?"

"Sid is leaving in two days, I will leave in about two weeks, right after my visa approval", I replied.

I turned and looked at him, he seemed a little more relieved. He looked at me and smiled. I bent over and hugged him. Abhi seems to be so much better when humbled and his ego crushed, I thought. So much more is felt than is said. I knew he would miss me but couldn't express it. I too was devastated to leave my family and country behind to go to a land I didn't want to go to.

——◆◆——

Sid was leaving for America. Holding me, he gave me assurance that everything will be good, that he will wait for me eagerly in California. After he left, I was confused and uncertain, but went with the flow without thinking much. It was so emotional at home, Mummy was packing everything immaculately, making sure I will have everything I need, Daddy was busy with all the logistics, while Abhi ran the errands. Soon we were off to the airport. I waited in the backseat of the car, while Daddy went to get the airport passes, and Abhi to get the cart and porter. Suddenly a tall, muscular, old man who looked like a beggar, put his head through the front window of the car and started telling me something, but I was too taken aback to register. With dirty, rag-like white clothes, and wearing a white headwrap, he held a long thick stick in his right hand. Shocked and startled, I initially could not register what he was saying.

After a few seconds I realized he wasn't begging but blessing me, and just heard the last part of what he was saying, "I will always be with you wherever you go, do not worry".

Then he blessed me with his right hand and walked away. I recovered from my frozen state and looked to see where he went, but I couldn't see him anywhere. It was as though he had disappeared. Much later, while looking at Shirdi Sai baba's photo in the book Mummy had given me, I realized that it may have been Sai baba.

Since then, I felt Baba's blessings and presence each time I was distressed, or at a major turning point in my life. It remains a mystery to me as to who it really was.

Hello California!

I felt a strange sense of knowing and comfort as soon as I landed in San Francisco. Sid was driving me from the airport to Palo Alto where he lived and worked. The clean crisp air, beautiful green hills, and the ocean bay, everything looked pristine. I loved the aliveness of the vibrations here. Palo Alto seemed like an older neighborhood, a university town with its famous Stanford University. Sid was doing his first year of fellowship in neurosurgery at Stanford Hospital. He drove past the University campus on our way to the faculty condos, my new home. The old Spanish architecture complex looked like a quaint urban oasis, with a central garden area and palm trees. Sid had just shifted to a two-bedroom rental. I was rather impressed with how clean, organized, and well equipped he had kept it. I realized immediately that he had an artistic side, a fine taste in furnishings, selected, unique pieces of handicraft items and classy home decor. He seemed happy and relieved with my praises, while being humble in receiving compliments. I was rather jet lagged, so I showered, had a quick meal and crashed well before nightfall.

In the early hours before dawn, in the twilight from sleeping to waking, I became aware of my dream. It felt vivid and real. I saw Sid and myself in what seemed to be a previous life. We were in Kashmir. Sid appeared to be a spiritual teacher or a priest. He was wearing a white garment with a gray shawl wrapped around him, and a *Tripundra* on his forehead - the three horizontal lines of ash worn on the forehead by followers of Shiva. He sat chanting some mantras with his eyes closed, his face so peaceful and radiant. I too sat near him, with my eyes closed, swaying to the rhythm of the chant. I could feel the vibrations as though I'm there in that life. I could sense that we lived in a humble log cabin, with sacred texts piled on a shelf, an altar, and an open kitchen in the corner of the hut. As I became more and more awake, thoughts covered the mind with a veil, and I lost the flow of the vision. Now I lay in bed next to Sid, suddenly realizing that I'm not in my parent's home in India, and the feeling that, oh my God! I'm in the US!

It was my first morning in a new American house, I had no clue about the kitchen, and the apartment was still a stranger to me.

Sid proceeded to show me where things were. "I drink coffee in the morning. Can I make you some *Chai*?" he asked.

I answered hesitatingly, "Sure, thanks. I will do it from tomorrow Sid".

"No problem, Lalla, take your time. I don't mind at all. We can do it together," he smiled casually and put me at ease.

Mummy had tried to teach me a few recipes and to help her in the kitchen, which is the last place I would rather be. Now I realized why she thought it was so important for me. Sid of course had been living independently in the US for so many years, so he could cook for himself.

After Sid left for work I felt so alone. There was pin drop silence, I could hear every little sound, even through the walls. When I went to the balcony, I could barely see anyone around. It was such a stark difference from the hustle and bustle of Bharat where there's constant activity from morning to night. The continuous flow of people in and around the house, from maids to *Sabzi Wallas* (vegetable sellers), so many sounds from people to traffic, and there is a sense of community and connection. Here it felt empty, silent, and dull. I was totally clueless as to what I would do all alone at home while Sid was at work. I couldn't drive here yet and there was no public transportation, so I was stuck at home. It would take me some time to adapt to married life and get integrated with the American way of living.

—— ❖❖ ——

Chapter 7

Soul's Cry for Justice

"**H**ey! Congratulations Karan. A CTO huh? Wow. So happy and proud of you," I said, elated that my college friend, Karan, had been promoted to a leadership role at a hot startup in Silicon Valley.

Karan and I sat outside a coffee shop on University Avenue in Palo Alto, catching up on things. Many of my classmates from our top engineering college in Bharat were here in the Bay Area, and we met periodically. Most of them were doing very well. It was January 19, 1990, and I had now been in the US for over a year, more integrated and enjoying living here.

Soon after I returned from meeting Karan, Sid came home looking rather disturbed.

I was putting away the groceries in the kitchen, when he sighed and said, "Shiv *Chacha* and his family narrowly escaped a deadly attack in Srinagar. The militants came for them, but they managed to slip away with the help of Dad's contacts".

I stopped abruptly and looked at him in disbelief. "Things are getting worse in Kashmir, Lalla. Dad was telling me that many Pandits are being murdered, women raped, and they are being threatened to leave Kashmir. Many of them have already left, leaving everything behind. The government isn't doing anything to protect them Lalla!"

I started thinking about my own family in Kashmir, wondering if they are safe.

At night I called my parents to ask out about our relatives. Mom picked up the phone and I briefly mentioned what Sid had told me, then asked about our family in Kashmir. She muttered a few words, couldn't get herself to speak, and handed the phone over to Dad. My heart started racing in fear of the worst.

Daddy spoke in a slow somber voice, "*Haan* Lalla, there's been some tragic events, Girija...," his voice started trembling, "Girija and Tina were leaving the medical college yesterday when her driver was with some militants who shot her...".

His voice weakened and went quiet.

"*Poff* was shot!" I screamed.

Sid rushed to hear what happened.

"She was taken back into the hospital, but those... those demons threatened the staff not to treat her or any

Hindus. So, she succumbed and...," he started sobbing softly.

"Oh my God!" I panicked, holding my forehead. "What about Tina *didi*?" I exclaimed.

"Tina was taken away by the terrorists, the police are searching," he said sadly.

"I can't imagine what they must have done with her! Oh my God, I can't believe this is happening!" I said, feeling pale in shock.

Sid took the phone from my hands and continued the conversation with Daddy, relaying what had happened with his uncle.

"Please talk to my father Daddy, I'm sure he can help," Sid said, concerned and worried.

I broke out in cold sweat, crying and feeling numb. Sid helped me lie down, then went to get me some water. He sat beside me, waving his hand through my hair, trying to calm me down.

"I want to go to Delhi Sid," I said weeping, "I want to be with my family. In fact, both of us should go. We both have lost our loved ones".

"Yes, we should. Let's plan that tomorrow," he replied somberly.

We barely slept that night, tossing and turning in despair. Our beings had suffered much trauma. I felt helpless being so far from my family, unable to do anything for them. I couldn't imagine how my family was coping in Bharat. My mind froze when I thought of Tina *didi* (my cousin). She had to see her mother shot dead in front of her eyes and then be kidnapped. I couldn't bear to think of what evil would fall on her. I sighed and squirmed with pain in my heart.

Sid hugged me from behind, whispering, "Rest now, we have much to do tomorrow."

The scene at Sid's parents' home was grave when we arrived in Delhi. Papa, Sid's father, was very busy meeting people constantly coming and going, and his home office had become like a war room. There were refugee camps being organized in Jammu where most of the Pandits who escaped from Kashmir reached. Some managed to come to Delhi. It was a mass exodus of our Kashmiri Pandits, like being invaded by the barbaric Turks and Mughals again. Yet I was experiencing this now; it was unbelievable.

Next day I went to Mummy and Daddy. Abhi had also arrived from London to be with the family. Our parents were in mourning. Some relatives were over to console them, others came to condole. Later when we were alone as a family, Abhi and I had to hear the unbearable, that Tina was brutally slaughtered. My body froze, and my mind became numb. Mummy took me away to my room and gave me some homeopathic 'Aconite' for shock, then asked me to rest. Abhi and Tina were very close, and his reaction was more volatile. He broke out in rage, yelling profanities and vowing to avenge this murder. If he could, he would join the army and personally eliminate all the terrorists. Abhi argued with family members on who was responsible and the lack of response. When we had family members visit, we inadvertently talked about this crisis, and Abhi cursed the nexus between the terrorists, Pakistan, and the Kashmiri government. He yelled at me when I tried to intervene to give an alternative view. Abhi hung out with members of groups that were finding alternative ways of finding justice. He was fuming mad, and we were worried about him taking dangerous steps.

In contrast I had to process things internally.

I lay down thinking in anger and sadness, "*Why do Kashmiri Pandits have to be exterminated again and again? Seven massacres and exoduses over seven hundred years, again and again, the same pattern. We are peace loving, spiritual people. With this genocide and ethnic cleansing would any Kashmiri Pandits even remain? Or will the whole demographics of Kashmir become Muslim forever*".

I had moved away from the spiritual center a bit after my marriage, and now I felt determined to connect to the Source again. The purpose of my life was spiritual, and this event was a wakeup call, a calling to align with my own nature, *SwaDharm*. I felt a change in my energy, something I hadn't felt in a while, it was like moving from a delusional dream back to reality.

Right now, it was about crisis management, there was very little true information coming in, and in this blizzard many fake stories were being propped up. After a few days, I didn't want to just grieve or feel weak or apathetic. I wanted to do something about it and take some action. There was a surge of energy in me. I told Sid that we must help in some way, not just sit back, and watch this happen to us. We talked to Papa and asked him to give us some assignments where we could contribute. There were three colonies in Delhi where rooms and temporary shelters were being provided, *Jangpura*, *Kalkaji*, and *Malviya Nagar*. Sid and I were to go to Kalkaji and were given the contact of the coordinator there.

We sat in the front seat of a small truck taking supplies for the refugees. When we reached, it was heart wrenching to see Pandits living in such deplorable conditions, stuffed into small rooms, well below basic standards. Some of these people came from cultured, affluent families, yet everything was lost right now. They were barely able to survive. Despite their circumstances, they greeted us with a smile. We brought them blankets, rice, clothes, and other basic necessities. Sid talked to the men of the families and noted their needs and grievances. He gave directions to some of the government workers to change or arrange for what was requested.

I listened to the women folk and greeted the children. They got a chance to express their grief and trauma. If only I could heal them and bring back everything they had lost. Many of them described the horrors of cold-blooded murders, brutal rapes, and kidnappings. We were fortunate enough to go to these rescue homes many times to help however we could. I felt so connected to everyone, and it seemed as though I could heal them with my words and my hands felt warm when I placed them on a person with an intention of healing. Looking into their eyes, I could feel their pain. Kashmiri Pandits were known to be one of the most knowledgeable and refined ethnic groups of Bharat, just look at what we were reduced to now.

This was a turning point in my life, something that would change me forever. At night when alone in bed, I meditated to get guidance on what my role was in all this. The initial faint messages became clearer, these capsules of telepathic messages steered me towards the path of my purpose. It was time.

————◆◆————

After spending a few weeks in Delhi, in the chaos and crisis, Sid and I had to return to the US. In the first weeks after returning, I started writing down my thoughts, so I didn't lose the flow or impetus I had felt in India. My energy felt razor sharp and intense. I practiced yoga, Pranayama and meditation daily. In contrast Sid's energy was steadier and more sustained.

One of the first things I had to do was to understand Islam. I had started studying the Quran when I was in college from Mina, and I resumed investigating it in detail now. I went into great depths while understanding Islam and their prophet Mohammed, referring to scholarly articles, books, and talking to those who had studied Islam. There were many eye-opening facts about Islamic conquests, with horrific accounts of their plundering Bharat as well. The genocide of Kashmiri Pandits had been going on for hundreds of years over waves of attacks. I wanted to be unbiased in my research and give the benefit of doubt to things that seemed violent and barbaric. I was able to get in touch with some ex-Muslim authors who left Islam after deep study and introspection. They removed many doubts I had, like, could it be that the verses had been modified for political power. These ex-Muslims I talked to, lived in exile in the West as they had to leave their homelands in Pakistan and Iran due to attacks and death threats. My study was for my own clarity on the truth about Islam and Mohammad, not to convince anyone else.

In parallel, and in contrast, I also resumed my study of the Holy Gita and other texts at the Chinmaya Mission in the Bay Area. Sid also accompanied me, and we discussed the knowledge afterwards to clear our doubts. Surprisingly I was able to absorb a lot of knowledge at the same time from various sources. While meditating on the knowledge I would look for the deeper meaning and get some revelations to the hidden subtle layers of understanding. As my basic nature was of devotion, I would later just drop everything at the feet of Sri Krishn and surrender, and then feel the light of His Grace and blessings. My devotion for Krishn had evolved from the playful interaction with Gopal as a child, the adulation for Govinda as a teenager, to a connection with Sri Krishn as a Guru, Yogeshwar Sri Krishn. I don't know how people find any relief without faith and devotion; it was my armor of protection.

I was not one to be restrained by the boundaries of any belief system. I had to experience and realize the truth on my own. With a single pointed, firm, and sincere quest for the truth, as well as a pure heart that seeks, I feel a window opens and grace descends, bestowing the light of knowledge with love. A personal connection with that living consciousness reveals the hidden secrets of the ancients. We also need to be prepared for what comes our way once we ask. For the next several months I experienced what I would call a Niagara Falls of downloads from a higher realm. I suddenly became more intuitive, I could 'know', see clairvoyantly, and get answers as soon as I asked. It was not from my human mind, but I seemed to have opened a channel to my higher Self from where messages flowed. There were many videos, online information, and so on that just came my way, as though someone was coordinating it all. People I happened to meet coincidentally, quickly became my new spiritual friends and family. A vast new realm opened before me, which had always existed, but I had never known. Now it was a reality. It was a clear shift into a new chapter of my life.

Chapter 8

Dropping of the Veil

Sid was very sensitive to what I was feeling, and it seemed he mirrored my state because he was empathetic. Though most of my experiences were private to me alone, at night I used to share some of them in a summarized form and present the questions I still had. He often gave brilliant responses in a very matter-of-fact way. While I would search long and deep for more convoluted answers, he could give them to me instantaneously. Maybe it was his genes, his grandfather was a well-known Kashmiri mystic.Sid always surprised me with his innate wisdom and peaceful presence. Maybe it was his genes, his grandfather was a well-known Kashmiri mystic. While my personality was intense and I tended to think deeply, Sid was very simple, grounded, scientific, and lived the values of his family and tradition. Sid used to read books on Kashmiri Shaivism and write poetry that he shared with me occasionally. We did a short Shiv puja together almost daily. Though he was not spiritual, just an uncomplicated man who was very private about his inner world, we shared an unspoken bond and supported each other's individual path.

There was a local Indian TV channel we watched on weekends. One day there was an author and researcher named Walter Semkiw being interviewed about past lives. I was very intrigued by his investigations on the subject. He mentioned that much of his work was supported by a channel medium named Kevin Ryerson, who became famous when the Hollywood legend Shirley MacLaine used him to get messages from astral beings. Channel mediums are those through whom another soul or spirit can speak, therefore they only relay messages. It seemed weird and spooky but I had to investigate all about Kevin Ryerson, and this later became an opening to a whole new ecosystem of new age spirituality.

I signed up for a session with Kevin Ryerson and couldn't wait to experience it for myself. I had written down the questions I wanted to ask in order of priority. Kevin Ryerson called me and gave me an introduction to the session as we started. He would record the session for me to listen to later.

My first question was to find out why I was born as a Kashmiri Pandit and if it had any connection to the purpose of my life. Kevin's voice changed as another spirit named Ahtun Re started speaking. Ahtun Re, as I had read, was an ancient Egyptian priest from around

3000 BCE. I was both excited and nervous as I listened attentively to Ahtun Re speak through Kevin.

He told me, "Indeed! There is a connection and purpose of your being born into the ancient tradition of Kashmir. You will find your purpose once you recall and relive the abilities you had when you were once a saint in Kashmir".

A saint in Kashmir? Me?

I was in disbelief, so I asked, "I was a Kashmiri saint? When? and what was my name? Oh! and by the way, my name, Lalla, was the name of a famous Kashmiri saint".

Ahtun Re cleared his throat and continued, "It is not important for you to know which Kashmiri saint you were at this time. What is important is that you bring forth the same level of enlightenment in this life as that, which is why you have come. You will remember who you were very soon if you choose. It would be a tragedy if in this life you do not pull forth the states of enlightenment that your soul has already attained".

He also went on to tell me that I would become a modern mystic, and still integrate my worldly existence with the spiritual aspects of my life. That's exactly what Kashmiri saints and sages did, they had families, as Kashmiri Shaivism can be practiced by householders.

The internet boom was taking place in the Bay Area and as I was not an avid reader, I preferred audio-visual learning via YouTube videos and other platforms. One day after watching a video on Kashmiri Tantra, YouTube suggested a video titled, '*The Pleiadian Message - A wake up call for the family of light*'. It was an excerpt from a book made into a video. It talked about how a cosmic race called the Pleiadians had come back to help humanity through a transition at this time for humanity. It felt as though my soul woke up listening to this message that seemed to be for me. Extraterrestrial beings? Pleiadians? It was hard for me to absorb all of it, but the part that resonated the most with me was that many of us had volunteered to come here at this time of the 'Shift'.

I searched voraciously on the internet about Pleiadians, and the rest of the book from which the video was made. I came across many people, websites, books, channelers, as I walked into what seemed like another dimension of new age spirituality. One website I found that engaged my interest, had an excerpt from a book by Sal Rachele. It gave details about the human psyche, a spiritual view of the current world issues, and foretold many transformational events to come. He also channeled some higher beings. I managed to find his website and read a few of his books very quickly.

These external discoveries coincided with a shift and transformation I was also undergoing in my own life. My experiences were becoming quite supernatural. I could distinguish between the times when I was my worldly personality versus when my presence, my energy, and my being was in a higher state of consciousness. At times when I was counseling a friend or a relative, it felt as though the words were just flowing out of my mouth, and they weren't coming from thoughts in my mind, they were a spontaneous expression. One part of me was observing what I was saying with astonishment at the wisdom which I myself didn't know. Yet it seemed very natural and peaceful. I seemed to be more awake and energized when this flow of consciousness took over my more mundane existence. I had reached a point where I had a choice of either remaining in my lower personality or transitioning to a more awakened state. A decision I postponed for now.

In the days and weeks that followed I was able to retain a higher state of consciousness for longer periods of time, sometimes for several days, while going about my daily chores. My sleep patterns had changed though. I would not go into deep sleep consciously, but I could observe my body in deep sleep. I was also aware that I was dreaming while dreaming. What I came to know was called lucid dreaming. During meditation I would tend to go into a void very quickly, a state beyond time and space, so I used to come back after hours without knowing how much time had passed. I then started keeping an intention of coming out of meditation after a specific period of time.

Sid also noticed that my energy level was different, though he didn't verbalize it, but I could sense he knew. It was natural for me to observe people's thoughts and feelings. I could sense the energy of places and people. Often, I knew what was going to happen next, and it would. While watching or reading the news I could see blurry images of the truth behind the stories. When people talked to me about something important, and if I intended, I could see their subtle energy bodies. If a friend came to me asking for advice about their problems I could see the root cause, even if it was in their past life. Many times, when needed for someone's benefit, I could see into a possible or probable future, though when it would happen was often not fixed. I started helping my friends, family and those they knew. I was hesitant to do anything beyond this, and I did not want to do it as a business or make myself public. In our tradition, people would go to wise people to get advice and there were no commercial exchanges.

Our green cards had finally come and now I was faced with a choice of whether I wanted to get a job or continue with a spiritual family life. Sid and I discussed this, and he left it up to me to decide, as he said he would be able to support the family financially. He advised me to take my time and reflect and not be hasty, I would need to be convinced of the path I chose, so that I don't have regrets later. I pondered on this for many days. It was interesting that I could not use my intuition on myself that easily. Perhaps because I was attached to the outcome. If I did not work, what would I do with my life apart from being a good wife, raising my future children and taking care of the house? I was not such a traditional old-fashioned woman anyway. It seemed though that my calling was something else, but what?

Abhi came to visit us for a few weeks during the summer upon our insistence he do so. We were driving to Monterey, Sid and Abhi were sitting in the front seats, and me at the back. Somehow the conversation led to my recent experiences with Kevin Ryerson.

In my mind I was saying, '*No, no, no!* as I didn't want to talk about this in front of Abhi.

Sid summarized, "Basically it is another being speaking through him, similar to how we see a *Deva* speaking through someone in trance".

"What? You went to some guy doing some witchcraft! Are you crazy Lalla? He could be a total fake you know. What was the need anyway?" said Abhi in a wide-eyed stare, reacting dramatically as I expected. Then saying, "Totally mad," under his breath and shaking his head.

Sid just turned and looked at him and went quiet seeing the tension between the twins, polar opposite twins. I felt really awkward, uncomfortable, felt my heart sink, and energy dropped. I sat back in my seat with a long face.

Abhi had managed to bury my self-esteem down underground, this time insulting me in front of my husband! It ruined my outing to Monterey and I was quiet all the way.

Am I really mad and weird? I questioned myself. How come I'm the only one in my family and friends who gets into all this strange spiritual stuff? I wondered. Maybe I should really focus on pursuing a career like everyone else and not get into all this woo-woo stuff. I felt so alone and lost.

——◆◆——

Chapter 9

Aligning with my Purpose

I felt I had no guidance, no Guru, so I went to the local Sai Baba temple seeking help.

Sitting in front of Baba, his smiling face looking at me with compassion, I asked him like a little girl, '*Baba I need a Guru. I have no one for guidance. What is all this I am experiencing, and where am I to go?*'

Tears rolled down my cheeks as my heart melted and I surrendered completely to him. I closed my eyes and sat quietly.

I heard Baba's percept, '*Withdraw from without to within, in the seed of your heart a Guru lies…*'.

A faint message hard to transcribe into words. Then, from my mind's eye, I saw a crystalline light emerging from Baba and enveloping me. It felt like a benevolent blessing of Divine Grace. That beautiful, blissful, blinding light filled my entire being from head to toe. Then, it was as though my whole body dissolved into it, becoming just light. I sat for a while absorbed in this divine blessing of Grace, *Anugrah* as it's called.

As I opened my eyes, I felt these words emerge from my mind, '*Param Shiva is my consciousness, is everyone's consciousness, everything is different densities and forms of consciousness*'.

I looked around the temple hall and all I could see was forms of that Supreme Being pervading everything, like one giant ocean of consciousness. I felt different, my body felt different. Something I hadn't felt in a long time. Similar to the experience I had as a teenager, when I went into *Samadhi*. I felt so peaceful, my mind was silent. I bowed to Baba in gratitude and got up.

As I walked from the main hall to the *Dwarkamai* room, passing several people, I was in a different state, and a spontaneous poem rose from my heart.

In this crystal palace, I am a guest, from whose windows I see others walking asleep.

The same liquid light becomes me, becomes crystal, becomes all bodies I see.

When I close my eyes, all ends in a void. When I open them, there's an unending dream.

You are the Self within myself, a marriage as this is seen,

From one form to another we travel, yet separate we have been.

You remembered our union, and I forgot somewhere in between.

For the love of You I surrender and sacrifice my separate being

Returning to mySelf I realize, I forgot, I only remembered, and it is I alone that will play this play again unendingly.

———◆◆———

'*Within two years you need to be ready to do our work in the world. The earliest the Earth Shift will start is in two years. Time is being manipulated. Many changes are coming*'.

I heard this message and saw some visuals in meditation just before the new year. I need to be ready, but how? I had to follow my inner voice and guidance. Once I made the intention of connecting only to the highest and most beneficial, I came into complete alignment with my higher Self and trusted the flow. I knew that in some way I needed to help others, perhaps I should learn some techniques, and get some certifications and credentials for that.

Sid and I discussed whether I should join Stanford to do an MBA and get a job, or start my own venture with some friends. I told him that I would rather do spiritual work with people, and perhaps write, or create content. I would have to force myself to pursue an academic degree or corporate career, I told him. He listened attentively, was happy to hear that I had found some clarity of direction in my life, and gave me some practical advice. I felt grateful that he was so supportive. It relieved me from the fear of sharing something so unconventional, and he saved me from feeling guilty or scared to pursue what I really wanted to in my life.

I felt as though there wasn't much time and I had to hurry to learn as much as I could, as fast as I could. One of the things that fascinated me was past life regression (PLR). Brian Weiss' book, '*Many Lives, Many Masters,*' had become famous, and it was awe inspiring for me. I thought I would take a PLR first, and then perhaps train to lead them myself. I searched and scheduled a session with a therapist, Smita, who was trained by Brian Weiss, and practiced locally. In preparation, I had to write down the questions I had which Smita would pose to me during the session. I also had to describe the important relationships I had in my life, like my family and friends.

During the session, I was very comfortable and easily suggestable to be able to move into the past. The first past life I saw was with a man wearing white clothes and seemed to be a priest or a very knowledgeable spiritual teacher. I recognized this man's energy signature as being Sid's soul. I saw myself as his supportive wife as well as his student. Both of us lived in Kashmir. I had seen a vision of this past life a few times after I married Sid. Now I was seeing an extended version of that. We both pursued a life of spiritual service to others as a couple. We worked in tandem. There was a beautiful connection between us where we didn't have to say much to each other, we knew what the other was thinking. There was an unseen bond.

The next life I saw was where I seemed to be a mystic, or at least seemed to have mystical experiences. In the first scene I saw myself sitting next to a *chula* (an earthen stove) cooking, but had gone into a trance. When my husband called out for me, I arose out of that deep state and looked at him with a peaceful smile. My face was gleaming. He was not only very kind, loving and wise, but also had a lot of respect for me, as he knew I was a pure devout soul.

When Smita asked me to move on to another experience, I seemed to travel somewhere in space, or perhaps beyond space and time. I saw beings of lights as a collective who told me telepathically that they are an expression of the Source. At this time I went into a trance and the Source energy spoke through me to Smita.

Smita: "*Why was Lalla shown these lifetimes?*"

Source: "*She was shown these lives so that she would remember some of the abilities she has had so that she can bring them forth in this life. She was also shown lives where she and her husband have had a supportive relationship and a balance of the worldly and the spiritual*".

Smita: *"What is it that Lalla needs to do in this life? What is her purpose?"*

Source: *"She has chosen to come back to Earth to help others evolve and raise their consciousness at this time of transition on the planet. Something she chose to do before her soul incarnated. She is also connected to the Source, you all are, but for her it is a living experience. We are all connected, because we are all one, an extension and expression of Source. So she will help others remember their true Self, their higher Self and their connection to the Source".*

Smita: *"How can she help others? What exactly should she do?"*

Source: *"She will become a guide, she has a faint sense of that already. She has helped others raise their consciousness through her own technique in the past, which she will bring into her present existence in time to come. She can also ask us for help, we are always with her."*

Smita: *"Does she have a spirit guide or guides, and will she find a living guide or Guru in this life?"*

Source: *"She does not have a specific spirit guide or guides, but many ascended masters come in to give her the knowledge or abilities she needs at a particular time for a particular task. In this life she does not need a 'Guru', but because she feels more supported with one, she will find a realized master in the near future".*

Smita: "*Is there anything else you would like her to know, or any message you would like to relay to her at this time?*"

Source: "*She needs to trust her feelings, and know that she is ready to live her purpose. She needs to believe in her abilities and let them flow as she helps others. There are many people waiting to come into her life. As she enters into the next phase of her life she will join others who have come to the planet for the great shift when the inflection point is reached for the quantum leap into the next level of evolution*".

It took me some time to digest and integrate the messages from my PLR. The moment I made the choice to be in alignment with my soul and my purpose here on earth, I seemed to flow with the current of this huge ocean of existence. An invisible intelligent system seemed to put everything perfectly in place magically. I allowed my mind to trust this universal system and let go of my fear of change, of the invisible, the unknown, and unexplainable.

I wondered if Sid would understand my experience and was surprised with his take on it. He said that these experiences and knowledge were commonplace in the spiritual culture of Bharat, and that we were re-discovering it from a modern western perspective. Sid and I were planning a child, and were not very successful so far. He was also very busy at work with surgeries and clinics, and was away for long hours. Luckily I had enough to occupy myself with. We still managed to have a social life with a few groups of friends, and at least once a year we would escape for a nice holiday.

Meanwhile, Abhi had finally decided to get married to Sunanda, a girl who's family we knew and introduced him to about a year ago. I left for the wedding which was in two weeks, while Sid would join me closer to the wedding date. Abhi's courtship period was quite a contrast from mine, our parents barely had anything to do with Abhi's relationship except for the introduction. He was very firm about leaving our family out of his life and was not open to inputs. I had not gone for his engagement as it was only a month before the wedding. Even though I had met Sunanda in the past, I was privately curious about what would make such a beautiful person decide to marry him. He was not easy to have a relationship with. She would have to be very good natured, accepting, forgiving, tolerant, patient and adjusting. As I looked intuitively, I saw a scene of her crying, with Abhi shouting at her, and got a feeling they would break up in a few years after their wedding. That would be a difficult period for him and our family.

Abhi's wedding was mostly enjoyable, got to meet the whole family and close friends, but there were several unpleasant moments as well. He had many arguments with my parents, and created so much drama in the family. Nothing was good enough for him, he always felt something was lacking, and he had to have everything his way else he would hurl up a storm.

"Abhi, it's ok, why don't you compromise so that both yours and Mom-Dad's wishes are both fulfilled. It's not possible to have a half hour wedding ceremony, Vedic ceremonies have certain must-have components. How about this, let's talk to the *Brahmin*, and see if we can shorten it to one hour," I tried to intervene between a key contention point in the family about the wedding ceremony.

"Oh! Here we go! Lalla the family expert in Vedic rites and rituals! What, now you are going to add some of your voo-doo techniques and nonsense to my wedding as well?"

Abhi barked at me, placing his hands on his hips and staring into me, red faced and fuming.

Then he pointed his finger right at my nose and yelled into my face, "Just stay out of my wedding ok!"

My mom came quickly to put Abhi's hand down, and led him away from me into another room, pleading for him to calm down.

He defended himself and reverted with a lower voice, "Do you know she's training as some past life therapist? She's gone crazy. Why don't you drill some sense into her, to use her engineering degree and get a job, like her classmates. She's abnormal you know, something is wrong with her".

While my mom was still trying to talk him into cooling down, he stomped out of the room and walked past me whispering authoritatively, "Women are supposed to be seen not heard!"

I immediately wondered about the fate of the beautiful, intelligent and talented Sunanda who was about to become his wife. Interestingly, I could observe my mind and emotions remain mostly unaffected and detached, I was amazed. His silly chauvinistic drama was almost laughable. I kept mum with my internal chatter of observations and opinions for the remainder of the wedding. Abhi also got a talking from the elders, and controlled his tongue though each time he looked at me he had a stare.

Even though this time I didn't let Abhi's ego and arrogance scar my self-esteem, I really didn't want to be present in that negativity, so I was glad when it was over. Sid and I took a break to go on a short vacation to Udaipur, Rajasthan after which Sid returned to America. I loved Udaipur, and it felt so familiar, though I had never been there before. Last few days of my trip I also got a chance to spend some quality time with my beloved mom and dad, which was so nourishing for them after a stressful family wedding.

Back in the bay, I hit the ground running to continue with my learnings. In one year I completed my certifications in PLR, Yoga, sound healing (with a specialization in *Mantras*), became a trained *Pranic* (energy) healer, and a certified spiritual counselor or life coach. There were many things I studied in depth, like Ayurveda, Quantum Physics, Advaita Vedanta, Kashmiri Shaivism, advanced my study of the Gita, Islam, and many other topics. My approach was definitely scientific spirituality, integrating spirituality into our personality, and being pragmatic. I couldn't relate with spiritual people who seemed removed from reality.

There were many new age personalities whose videos, documentaries and books I studied on ancient civilizations, revelations about how the powerful elite control us (some say these are conspiracy theories), and future predictions about a shift in consciousness interested me the most. There were so many new age folks talking about aliens, their races, UFOs, and their role in our past and future. It seemed weird to me at first, but then I heard first hand stories from ordinary people as well which didn't seem fake. I also became part of many spiritual communities online and in-person, and started a group with people I knew where I lead yoga, chanting and guided meditations. Everything appeared to be moving at light speed, without obstructions. I could absorb ten different sources of knowledge in a day without being tired or overwhelmed. I was in a zone, with razor sharp focus, acting on my passion, and was excited. This was my authentic self, it was natural.

All the while Sid stayed in sync with me, I could share easily with him without hesitation. Sid was so different from Abhi. More than his adoration, I valued his genuine praise, admiration, and respect for me. However; some of our friends seemed to fall away or become distant. I couldn't talk to them about my life as they wouldn't be able to relate, nor could I with theirs. I didn't feel comfortable socializing with them anymore, it felt so trivial, fake and illusionary. There were some relatives who had a toxic attitude which was not beneficial for me. While in the past I forced myself to engage with them, going forward I maintained a cordial yet distant relationship. I found it extremely challenging to have a conversation with Abhi, as his pungent negativity came through his voice on the phone, and affected my entire being. I developed a much better relationship with Sunanda who had a pleasant presence. It was also difficult to listen to the news or shows on TV which focused mostly on bad things, and felt like it was like a narrative to condition or program our minds. I heard a lot of discussions on social media from different sources and perspectives about what was happening in our world.

I loved watching spiritual content on Gaia.com, it was like the juice of life for me.

There were many magical and mystical moments in my life as I shifted into a reality that had a different vibrational frequency than say the mass shootings on the nightly news. I found such amazing personalities whose existence I was unaware of till I became interested in these subjects. One of the communities I had joined was the International Association for Near Death Studies (IANDS). I loved going to their monthly events and listening to people who not only had Near Death Experiences (NDEs) but also gained spiritual abilities, realized their purpose, and had a complete shift in their lives. There were others like Anita Moorjani and Eben Alexander that had become famous after publishing books about their NDEs.

As I had completed my certification in PLR, I had started practicing this initially with my friends. I noticed that those who meditated had much richer experiences. There were some folks from my meditation group that had amazing sessions and also experienced healings. Many people had questions about death, the after-life, re-birth, and the dimension where souls exist. It was easy for me to explain things in these topics, I wondered why, till I realized that I seemed to have a specialization in the occult, esoteric and mystical subjects. Even my Vedic birth chart indicated that as per an astrologer.

I had got my Vedic birth chart read when a friend of mine insisted I do so with this astrologer he said was extremely accurate. I asked the astrologer about my past to ascertain his proficiency, and was really surprised when he gave mostly correct information. There weren't any burning questions I had but I did ask him if and when we would have children. He pulled Sid's chart as well and told me that chances were low of us having children, and gave me some remedies, prayers and such. The astrologer also told me to chant *Mantras* for Sid as he would go through a difficult period in a couple of years. He said that even though there were some rough patches, my future was quite promising, and that I had the leadership qualities if I chose to take on that role. Well we'll see, there was an interaction between destiny and free will, so the future was about possibilities and probabilities. On a deeper level, I felt this session wasn't just a coincidence but also a message about where our lives were headed.

It was as though there was a fork in the road, and not just for me, but for humanity as a whole. I had taken one path that was to evolve to a more positive future, and a new world of like minded folks seemed to open up. While another set of people had chosen another path that led to self destruction and negativity, and these people faded away from my life. Two possibilities, two worlds, two trains leaving in separate directions, utopia and dystopia. We had to choose quickly and board the right train, the whistles had blown, the trains were about to leave the station.

Chapter 10

Stepping Into a New Realm

Sid was sitting strumming his guitar singing a beautiful old Hindi movie song. Some of our close friends were over for dinner and we were enjoying this after dinner entertainment. Sid was of course a good singer, and a poet. Another friend, Anu, followed suit and sang another favorite with Sid accompanying her on the guitar finding the chords impromptu.

"That was amazing Anu!" I exclaimed as everyone clapped.

"Come on Lalla, you should sing a *Bhajan*. You sing them so well," said Anu.

I laughed and said, "Another day".

"Hey, you guys are going to Mt. Madonna next weekend right?" asked Jameel.

"Yah, looking forward to that. Need a break," Sid replied, putting away his guitar.

"I've heard it's such a peaceful place. My friend did his yoga course there. I would love to go there sometime," Jameel said.

"And it has a beautiful Hanuman temple, set on the hill, just like the temples in the Himalayas," I added, getting up.

All our friends helped us clean up and load the dishwasher before leaving.

The following Thursday Sid and I were off to Mt. Madonna retreat center for three nights to take the Kriya initiation course being given by spiritual master Sri M. One of my friends, Savitha, had read his book, *'Apprenticed to a Himalayan Master,'* and had already taken the Kriya initiation from him the previous year. As she highly recommended Sri M, I watched his interviews on YouTube, and I could sense he was a genuine master. Sri M belonged to the lineage of Sri Guru Babaji, also known as Maha Avatar Babaji of Paramahansa Yogananda. Therefore, the Kriya technique of Sri M and Yogananda is the same, or very similar. However; Sri M and his Guru Maheshwarnath Babaji were part of the 'Nath Sampradaya', which is a spiritual tradition or lineage that descends from the Navnaths, Dattatreya, and Adi Nath (Shiva). Sri M, I found out, was very knowledgeable. He had also studied Kashmiri Shaivism and met Swami Lakshmanjoo. As I was still a keen *Krishn bhakt* (devotee), it wasn't the Kriya initiation that excited me, it was spending time with a realized master that attracted me.

The drive to Mount Madonna center was beautiful as we drove through the evergreen forest up the coastal hills. My spirit was lifted as soon as we reached. It was one of my favorite places. Tucked in the hills, amongst tall evergreen and redwood trees, this spiritual sanctuary overlooked the Monterey bay, a beautiful view. On the hillside was the Hanuman mandir (temple), which was built by Baba Hari Das who was a disciple of the great saint, Neem Karoli Baba. The temple resembled the Hanuman temples in and around Neem Karoli Baba's ashram in Kainchi near Nainital in the foothills of the Himalayas.

After paying our obeisance at the temple to Sri Hanuman, we checked in and were given a room in the conference center where the meditation center for the course was located. Savitha and her husband also came and checked in and we all went to the dining hall for dinner. After dinner there was a welcome and initiation session in the meditation hall. Sri M briefly came in to talk to us and gave us a rough outline of the course. He seemed so modest and sweet, no fuss, no trail of devotees. He was wearing plain clothes, pants and shirt, not the typical outfit of Hindu Gurus. It was a small group of us, less than a hundred, which he wanted, and so he wasn't into increasing his followers. He made eye contact with all of us and after the session he walked by and talked to several of us individually. We just did *Pranams* as he walked by us as we didn't have any questions. Many of us stayed behind and minged. We met some very nice people who had come from all parts of the country, and we all shared our spiritual stories. The vibrations of Mount Madonna had set in and we went to sleep in so much peace.

One the first full day of the course Sri M gave us some foundational knowledge in the tradition of *Kriya Yoga*. He also taught us the 'Hum-Sau' *Pranayama* or *Kriya* (the precursor to the ultimate *Kriya* technique). He said that this 'Hum-Sau' technique was more than enough for those who were ready, and that collecting techniques is not necessary, but then assured the eager ones that he will give us the *Kriya* for which we came.

The next day we sat early waiting to be initiated into the secret and mysterious *Kriya*. There was pin drop silence as he started giving us an introduction to the *Kriya*. One of the central aspects in Kriya Yoga is the Kundalini Shakti and the seven Chakras. The Kundalini is represented as a coiled serpent that lies dormant at the base of the spine. With Kriya Yoga this Shakti (energy) can be awakened, and with practice this serpent-like energy can slowly rise up the seven chakras to the top of the head. Sri M also explained the Kriya procedure, as we all listened attentively, while some were writing down notes.

Sid and I were sitting somewhere in the middle of the hall. Sri M first demonstrated all the steps that are followed before and after the *Kriya* technique. Then we practiced it together for the first time. During the *Kriya* our eyes were closed, and at one point I felt a ray of energy emanate from Sri M and enter my forehead (the third eye). It felt sort of like a gentle electric current that traveled through my body. I didn't think of it then but pondering on this later I realized that this is what is perhaps called the '*Shaktipat*', a spiritual initiation by the way of transmitting spiritual energy from one being to another. After the *Kriya,* with my eyes still closed, I felt my energy shoot up, as though I was about to have an out of body experience.

In the meditation after the Kriya, I saw a golden light between my eyebrows (the third eye). Then I seemed to surge or travel with this ray of light outward into space reaching a grand light form like the sun. I was inside this golden globe of light which seemed like a living being communicating with me. After sometime I receded with the golden ray back into my body. Soon after this the meditation ended. As I opened my eyes slowly I saw a golden glow everywhere. Though I could also see the physical bodies and objects, everything was filled with different densities of golden light. Even the space between objects was filled with flowing scintillating golden light. I winkled a few times but it remained. When I looked at

Sri M there was a huge aura of golden light around him, and a silver apparition that overlapped his physical body. I interpreted that as the presence of Sri Guru Babaji. His face had a brilliant glow and I could barely look at him. I don't think anyone else could see this except me.

People were asking some questions, and some shared their experiences. Sid turned and looked at me to gauge my experience, but my mind was silent and I was still mesmerized. When the session was over and I stood up, I had so much energy that I felt a bit 'high'.

Sid was finally able to ask me, "How was your experience?"

"Brilliant...amazing!" I replied, "How was yours?"

Sid smiled and said casually, "Felt very nice... peaceful".

I still kept seeing this golden light everywhere as we walked to the dining hall. While we were having lunch I told Sid about my Kriya experience and he said I should share it with Sri M. It was good to have lunch and feel more grounded.

We had more sessions in the day but we ended early, so after dinner all the participants got together for a spontaneous *Kirtan Satsang* in the veranda outside the meditation hall. Sid played his guitar. I was relieved to finally go to bed. At night I seemed to go on an astral travel. Everyone travels out of their bodies into astral realms while they sleep, we just don't remember it. However; this time I was aware. I traveled out into space in the form of a little girl, and there I met Sri M who appeared as a gray serpent with yellow eyes. We had a telepathic conversation. Out into space there was a realm with different hues of blue. Perhaps that was Narayan's Vaikunth Lokh? I pointed in that direction and pleading like a child, I asked Sri M to take me back there.

Sri M looked at me with compassion and said, *"What do I do with you?"*

I kept looking at him in anticipation. That vision ended there and I returned to my body awareness. In the morning I shared my experience with Sid, and wondered what he would make of it.

"Don't discount it Lalla. I suggest you ask Sri M. He's the master. Don't hesitate, this is your chance".

It was the last day, we were back in the hall, and Sri M was seated in front starting the session. As I had a few times before in my life, I could see his astral body through his physical body. What I saw was the same gray serpent with yellow eyes! The astral body is translucent and fills the space within the frame of the body. His astral form of the serpent was so prominent that it made me uncomfortable. Was I hallucinating? I knew that the *Nath* Gurus of the *Nath Sampradaya* were associated with Nagas, i.e., serpents. In his autobiography,

Sri M had mentioned this association. The Kundalini is of the form of a serpent, and in the masters whose Kundalini had fully risen, this etheric serpent can perhaps be seen. During the Q&A session I asked Sri M to tell us about the *Nath Sampradaya.* He was so happy to explain it to us.

Afterwards when we lined up to take his blessings one by one, he smiled and blessed me saying, *"Alakh Niranjan!"* [Alakh Niranjan is a term used by Nath yogis to describe the Supreme]

I wanted to confirm if my vision of the serpent form I was seeing was for real, so after the session I followed him out of the hall to the exit door.

I called out to him, "Sri M...".

He turned around and stopped.

I asked, "Sri M, are the *Naths* associated with *Nagas?*"

He looked at me for a second, then laughed, saying, "Do you see me as a *Naga?*"

I replied fervently, "Yes! yes! I do! I can only see you as a *Naga*".

He said jokingly, "And what if I hiss?" and walked away towards his car.

Ah! For me he had just validated that what I was seeing was real and I was not hallucinating.

I went running to Sid to tell him about my exchange with Sri M. I was so excited and he was so happy. What a wonderful end to an extraordinary course. I did not realize it immediately but over the next many days, a realization slowly and gently opened up within me. Was it that Sri M had just played the role of a Guru for me? Was the energy transfer I felt the Kripa or Anugrah (divine grace) that I had read about in books? Was it divine grace that gave me the vision of the golden light, the astral travel, and the subtle serpent body of Sri M? Had I just been initiated by my Guru? Wow, what a revelation! Sri M, I found out, was in the Bay Area for some private meetings and events, and I had to meet him again. Over the last few years I had started writing articles for spiritual websites and local newspapers, and was keen on interviewing Sri M to reveal this hidden jewel to sincere seekers who were looking for guidance. I contacted Sri M's local coordinator, Naresh, and got an appointment to interview him in a few days. I was thrilled, to say the least, and a bit nervous as well. I gathered a list of questions from seasoned spiritual aspirants and had to add some of my own. That night, when I was thinking of what questions I would ask, I felt Sri M's presence come into my room through the window like a bubble and then next to me. I wondered if it was really him. Then he told me (telepathically) that he had a surprise for me when I would come.

On the day of the interview Sid and I arrived at Naresh's home in Silicon Valley. Sid would assist me by being the cameraman. We were doing a live event on social media and had spread the word about it. Sri M came out from his room wearing casual clothes, we greeted each other, and he remarked that he remembered me from the course. He was so humble and treated us as his equal, with no airs about being a realized master. He and I sat on either side of the cough and we began our conversation. It was a very engaging exchange, and I was focusing on understanding his answers. In one of his replies he started narrating a story about the musk deer by the famous saint Kabir of the fifteenth century. As I was looking at Sri M and it happened again. Within the frame of his body, I saw another man, and instinctively I knew it was Kabir. I was not astounded or distracted, in fact I took it with the flow of his narration, and continued with the rest of the interview without anyone knowing what I had just witnessed. After the camera was off I asked Sri M a couple of other questions that I didn't want recorded, one being about ancient civilizations and Naga Lokh. He told me briefly that he had experiential knowledge of an ancient age as he had astrally traveled to this time that existed prior to the ice age. I wanted to know more, but he had to leave for an appointment so he asked me to come back and continue the conversation. We thanked him, touched his feet and left.

On the drive home I told Sid about my experience, and wondered if Sri M was Kabir in a previous life, or was it Kabir who came within him to channel the story. Soon after reaching I messaged Naresh to give me Sri M's personal email as I wanted to ask him a question. I then emailed Sri M right away relaying the experience I had, asking him if he was indeed Sant Kabir in his previous life, and requested a confirmation on whether I should trust my intuition.

He replied to me the next day saying, "Excellent intuition. Love and blessings. M".

I was so happy to receive his reply, and even though he worded it carefully, I knew he was giving me the validation I seeked. He was seasoned enough to know not to specially say in writing that he was a famous saint in his previous life, that would stir controversy. I tried to meet him again to continue our conversation but it didn't happen then, and I hoped that the right time would come in the future.

❖

Chapter 11

A Second Life

I had read a book titled, *'Journey of Souls,'* by Michael Newton and was awed by the knowledge revealed in that book. Michael Newton was a regression therapist who cataloged three thousand cases of people he regressed and took them to a state in which the soul is in-between lives. It also talked about the process of a soul choosing the next life. The sections of the book went from junior souls to advanced souls, and most of the times the higher Self of the person, or higher beings spoke through the person during the session. I was keen on experiencing this myself and found a local practitioner and signed up immediately.

At the session Susie, the therapist, explained that I would be taken to the last day of a past life, and go through the passing away process. Then I would start my journey after life into other realms. This session would be to see the experience of the soul before the soul takes the next incarnation. After Susie regressed me, I started seeing images.

Susie: "Where are you now and what do you see around you?"

Me: "I believe I am a Tibetan monk. I am lying down in bed, in a small dark hut. I am old and about to pass. I see incense burning and there are two younger monks on either side of my bed chanting. I have taken myself into deep meditation to unite with my soul as it passes out of the body. [Pause] Now my soul is leaving the body and going up, higher and higher. I am now in an astral realm being bathed with a purified light to remove any impressions and heal me. [Pause] I see two queen angels, umm, wearing translucent flowing gowns and a crown. They come to receive me and flood me with immense…[sigh] divine warm motherly love. It's *so* much love, it's hard to describe.

Now I am going through a whirling tunnel, like a wormhole. I've popped out to the other side. A very expansive realm. I'm like a little child, feeling free and happy to be home. I'm flying around fast, here and there. [Pause] I've come to an area in space which is like a library. I'm asking a question, and I see some knowledge encoded in light coming up through space, like rising from a well. It's a question I had when I was alive that I didn't get an answer for, '*What's the structure of creation?*' I am being shown the structure of space or creation as different geometric patterns made up of light, one on top of another".

During the session I saw many things about my soul in the in-between life states which included seeing my soul group, my soul's role in creation, soul's nature, and many masters. Susie also took me into the future, at which point I felt I started channeling from my higher Self.

Me: "I see that in the coming year there will be what seems like a war in which many people will die. I also see a lot of children dying. [Pause] We will then enter a twenty year transition, of which the first seven to eight years will be tough and transformational. [Pause] I think I am seeing something after this transition. I see myself as a Being outside the planet's atmosphere. I am connected to other beings in sort of a grid with other souls".

Susie: "How many of you are there?"

Me: "A hundred and forty four thousand (144,000)".

Susie: "What's happening on the planet?"

As I looked with my mind's eye I replied, "Everything seems to be destroyed somehow, I see burnt structures and ash everywhere".

"Is there anyone left surviving?" she asked.

"Only a few people," I responded.

It was just a mind blowing experience and it took me sometime to resettle into the present and get grounded. Susie and I talked for sometime after the session discussing various spiritual topics and then I came home. She told me that the 144,000 is mentioned in the last chapter of the Bible called Apocalypse or Revelations. It is from the twelve thousand (12,000) from the twelve (12) tribes of Israel who will have a role to play during a great transition that's mentioned in this chapter of the Bible.

Sid was always happy to hear my stories after my spiritual escapades and was a patient listener. I was so lucky! Perhaps he treated me lovingly like a little girl, who got excited by such experiences.

"But Sid, I saw something terrible for next year, like a war, and many people were dying," I said concerned.

"If it's meant to be, it will be. We can only handle it to the best of our abilities at that time. No one can really prepare for such things. Let's hope for the best Lalla," said Sid very calmly.

What was I to know of what was coming, and how it would change the world and my life forever. In March of next year the whole world started battling a disease no one was prepared for, and for which there was no medical remedy. Sid and I were in the center of it as Sid still continued his practice at Stanford Hospital and Clinics. He and all medical workers were the front line soldiers in this battle. The COVID virus was spreading like wildfire, and the media fanned the fears even more. This was an unprecedented time, no one living on the planet had faced such a health catastrophe. The numbers of the dead kept rising, and the deceased suffered a most tragic death of dying alone without family members, and the last rites also done without full involvement of loved ones.

Sid had moved into a separate bedroom and worked long hours. We took massive amounts of precautions to protect ourselves. I was very worried about Sid, his family wanted him to quit, and his poor mother was so anxious. There was no avoiding it in the hospital, one after another, people in his department got sick with COVID, some recovered, others critical and a few didn't win the battle. Even though I was brave mentally, my body subconsciously wasn't able to cope. I got panic attacks if I suspected Sid caught COVID. My spiritual evolution was tested to see how much I had truly detached, and if I had integrated the truth within. I took many steps back, and realized that this is the time to practice and realize the words of the Gita. I had to also be an example to others who were living in so much fear of death, as I looked to my role models like Sri M and other spiritual masters.

Just when I felt I had finally gained some inner anchoring in detachment and wisdom I was put to the test again. Sid didn't come home one day, I kept waiting and calling him but no answer.

Late at night I got a call from his head of the department saying quite matter of factly, "Hello Ms Kashyap, hope you're doing well, this is Mark from Sid's team. Just wanted to let you know that Sid was showing some possible COVID symptoms and we would like to isolate him here till his COVID PCR test results came back. So he's been admitted. It should be at most a couple of days. I know this sounds very worrying, but really we are being extra cautious, and we shouldn't assume anything at this point. Sid is doing really well otherwise".

"Oh no! Yes, this is definitely worrying Mark. Thanks for calling me, I was wondering where he is, and was concerned as I couldn't get in touch with him. Anyway, keep me posted please, I will be eagerly waiting to hear the results".

"Sure, will do. I know these are difficult times, and trust me, we are taking good care of him here. You take care!"

———◆◆———

Day 1: I tried to keep calm and asked the floor nurse if I could chat with him on a video call, and I did. I knew Sid, he would act normal and not want to show any signs that would make me perturbed.

He smiled and said, "I'm feeling a little tired. Just need to rest. How are you? Please don't worry, I'm doing good. Let's wait till the result comes. One day at a time. Just keep this from mom-dad as I don't want them to panic".

"Of course, I won't tell them. Did you get good sleep, and have you been eating ok?" I was somewhat concerned.

"Yes, I asked for some tylenol for my body pain and then I could sleep for a good six hours. Had a good breakfast".

We talked for a little bit, said he felt tired and just needed to rest. Sid assured me that he was in good hands and will be well taken care of, all will be well, and not to worry. That's all we spoke.

After our conversation, I paced up and down not knowing what to do. I sat down to chant and pray to calm myself down. Then I had to gather the courage to call and tell my parents. I talked to Daddy first and told him about Sid. We decided not to tell Mummy right now till the results come, as she would needlessly be disturbed all the while.

In the meantime Abhi's wife Sunanda became pregnant, and that too would be a rather challenging pregnancy during COVID. I spoke to Abhi and Sunanda over the phone to congratulate them, however it was a bittersweet moment for me, considering that Sid was unwell. I refrained from telling Abhi anything about Sid.

Day 2: I couldn't get myself to sleep most of the night, till I realized I have some homeopathic medicine my mother gave me to calm my nerves and help me sleep. Early next morning I got a call from the nurse to give me an update that he slept well and would speak to me around lunch time. When we talked over a video call I sensed he was weaker and could talk less.

He said, "I am doing ok, just feel very weak".

I knew he wasn't telling me everything, as there was nothing I could do about it and the anxiety would really affect me.

I didn't want to show him that I was already anxious, so I tried to smile and make him feel positive, "Can't wait to have you back home Sid and make some of your favorite dishes. Hang in there, get better fast!"

Much later I had come to know that he was now running a fever, had a headache, and all the other symptoms of COVID. I could not speak to him again in the evening as they said he had gone to sleep, and was given some tylenol to help him with the body aches. It was another long night for me, and a difficult conversation with Daddy again. Everyone else in the family was still in the dark.

＊＊

Day 3: The COVID test results were going to come today so I called the nurse to ask in the morning. When I saw Sid now over video, they had put an oxygen mask on him as he was having some difficulty breathing and his oxygen count was a little bit lower. I knew at this point that he probably did have COVID, my body became cold with fear. He managed to speak a few sentences softly, saying he loves me, to be strong and tell his parents not to be scared, all will be well. As a doctor he knew what was going on and how this could get worse. Like an injured soldier he had to keep up the fight with all his will.

Late afternoon I got the bone chilling news that the COVID test had come positive, it was just a stamp on what we all had already suspected. I felt numb and couldn't really register what had just happened. I chanted and prayed with all my heart, then dropped on my knees and cried. The only thing I could do is surrender. I did have faith, and that helped me cope with the fear. This was a big lesson in my life, to keep my emotions and thoughts in balance, and do whatever it takes to calm my anxiety. Some pranayamas, meditation and homeopathic remedies helped. Now I could call his parents and convey the news.

I spoke to Papa first, who handled it very maturely and said he will convey this to Sid's mom himself so he can handle her reaction. In a little while the phone rang and Mom wanted to talk to me herself.

"I know you are also alone and have to handle this all by yourself. What can we do, we just have to be brave and support one another," she said sadly and we both cried.

I was alone at home, while they had each other at least. My parents had to know too, so I had another emotional conversation with them. I also called a couple of our closest friends in whom I could confide and get support. It was a surreal day, I put on some *bhajans* and went to sleep emotionally exhausted.

———— ◆◆ ————

Day 4: After a few hours of sleep I waited till dawn so I could call the nurse to see how Sid was doing. He had a difficult night and they had increased his oxygen level to help him breathe. I couldn't talk to him and had to wait towards the end of the day to get another status update. The nurse said he was stable during the day, and had managed some oral food, though he was coughing a lot. After giving both sets of parents the daily update, I went to bed anxious, and I couldn't put myself in his shoes to feel the dire physical state he was in. It was important for me to get some rest as I knew the next day would be long and difficult, so I took something to help me sleep.

———— ✦✦ ————

Day 5: I was still groggy in the early morning hours when I got a call from the doctor. He said that they had to put Sid on the ventilator as his condition became critical in the middle of the night, and said that his chances of survival are slim, that they were trying their best, but I should be prepared for the worst. It was hard for me to register and process as my mind wasn't yet awake or clear.

I fell back in bed rather disturbed, and after tossing and turning a few times thinking, '*I need to get up and call Dad. Oh! my God! What's going to happen now? Om Namah Shivaya, Om Namah Shivaya, Om Namah Shivaya…*', and I drifted into a deep sleep.

After a couple of hours I got up with a jerk, as I had fallen asleep, and with the sudden realization that Sid was critical, on a ventilator and I may lose him! Oh my God! My heart pounding, I checked my phone and saw a couple of missed calls from the hospital. I immediately called the floor nurse. My body tightened and my face froze as I was expecting to hear bad news, but the nurse was rather calm, so I relaxed a bit. Then I asked for a status and a few questions to understand exactly what his condition was, if it was stable and getting better or worse.

She surprised me by saying that he was stable and in a much better state now, and they would take him off the ventilator later today to see if he can breathe on his own. I hung up the phone feeling confused and in disbelief at this sudden positive turn of events. I couldn't absorb it all yet. I wished and prayed it would continue in this direction. It would be in the middle of the night now in India so I couldn't tell our parents yet.

Early that evening the doctor called me for the first time to give me an update. He was happy to report that Sid was taken off the ventilator and was breathing normally for the last couple of hours. Phew! What a relief. He said that Sid was really a fighter and had an unbelievable recovery, which they rarely see. It was truly a miracle. I asked him what I should expect now over the next day or two. He said that they would monitor him over the next two days and if all his vitals are stable, then he should be out of danger, and hopefully within a week he would test negative for COVID.

I was so happy and excited that I cried over the phone telling our families, "Sid is actually astonishingly recovering! All our prayers were being heard Ma. We should continue them till he is fully and completely out of COVID".

There was so much joy and celebration in our families in India. It was the first night in a week that I could actually sleep without a disturbed mind. What a lesson this had been for me in my spiritual journey. How much more I had to actually live the knowledge, and not be so disturbed no matter what the situation. I feel I have completely failed. Why was it so difficult to overrule the mind with wisdom? I had to practice this more and more, I had to learn this once and for all.

———◆◆———

Day 6: I woke up well rested and the nurse told me she would do a video call with Sid after he had his breakfast. I saw Sid as if I was seeing him for the first time after ages. His eyes sparkled as he smiled. He seemed fresh and alive, as though he was born again with a new life. He was still coughing so didn't speak much, but he calmed my fears and told me that he felt absolutely fine. What a blessing! I noticed a difference in his energy and presence, but maybe it was because he had gone through so much. I wondered if he had an NDE (Near Death Experience) and then brushed that thought aside. That day I was so happy I skipped and twirled and danced. The dark night of the soul was behind us and this was a new day and a new beginning.

The next few days Sid recovered easily and fully. They kept him in isolation for some more days till finally his COVID test came negative. It was like we have won the war and the POW has been released. After a total of two weeks in the hospital he finally came home. I ran out to the parking lot when he arrived in the ambulance.

"Welcome home Sid! Oh my God! You're finally home," I laughed and cried at the same time, and put my arms around his neck.

Sid was still weak, but happy and smiled and he bent over, gave me a hug, then we went inside. It was a celebration with just him and me, as the whole world was 'sheltering at home'.

Finally I could interact with him in person, give him home cooked food, and he could rest in his own bed. There was a difference about him that seemed more pronounced now than what I had noticed after his miraculous recovery from the ventilator. I looked into his eyes and felt as though it was someone else, and almost wanted to ask him, "*Who are you?*" But I held back my words as they would be too far out, and may not even receive an answer. At night in bed he murmured a few strange things like he's glad to be here now with me, what time I wake up and where his things are. I found it a bit odd, but perhaps COVID had disoriented him. I wanted to inquire how come he doesn't remember, but he sighed and closed his eyes to rest. His body was still very weak and I postponed this conversation for a later time.

The next day I contacted a psychic medium, Bonni, whom I'd talked to in the past, and luckily got an appointment for later that week. A psychic, a clairvoyant, or a medium is someone with advanced intuitive abilities who can access information that can't be gained by an ordinary mind. I eagerly awaited our conversation, and wrote down questions that came to mind. My opening statement was about Sid's COVID recovery, and I described how I felt about this strange difference in his presence and personality. Did he have an NDE? Or an awakening or what exactly?

Bonni is a very gentle, sweet and compassionate soul, and even though she explained softly, I was rather taken aback by her answer. I didn't expect it at all. She said, what she sees is that Sid went through a death and rebirth process and it resulted in a 'walk-in'.

"He's a walk-in!" I exclaimed, a little shocked.

I knew what the term meant. She confirmed and conveyed that Sid's soul exited the body when he was on the ventilator, and, as agreed previously with another soul, let this other soul enter into this body at this time. So there was a soul exchange.

"Who is he? I mean who has walked-in?" I asked with my curiosity soaring.

Bonni replied, "He's really the soul you were meant to be with at this time, for the transition humanity is going through. Sort of like your soul companion. All three souls involved here had chosen this before birth.

Also this soul is sort of a higher version of Sid's soul, as they are from the same lineage. You will support each other as a pair, energetically, to accomplish the tasks you have come here for".

"Wow!" I said, astonished.

"He's not a stranger to you, as you have known him from before, you may feel a familiarity," she assured me.

"I...I don't know. I can't put my finger on it, and couldn't really gain clarity or understanding on what I feel about him," I said, a bit confused.

"Give it some time, and just feel it from the heart, the answers will come to you," she guided me.

We set up another session in a few months.

I had to mull over all the things Bonni told me. Though the concept of a 'walk-in' might seem strange to some, it has really been known by different terms over the ages. In primitive and tribal cultures there have been shamans, healers and priests who deal with spirits and souls that may enter someone to trouble that person. In recent times also this notion of spirit or deity speaking through someone is common in many places around the world. Getting messages from higher beings in conscious or meditative states also has familiarity amongst spiritual seekers. In India many masters have had special abilities to deal with this topic of spirits, soul, and ascended masters.

There are at least a couple of famous Indian spiritual masters who consciously did a walk-in to another body, Adi Shankaracharya and Tirumular. The body is a vessel and the soul is an energy capsule, and there can be more than one energy influencing a body.

In the session Bonni helped me to accept the situation and ease into it. Her insights gave me a better in depth and comprehensive understanding. After the conversation, my energy was high and drained at the same time. I took a nap which made me feel a bit more balanced. I sat at the edge of the bed, facepalm, feeling jittery about how I would interact with Sid, suddenly a complete stranger to me. When he came in the evening I tried to behave normal and didn't make eye contact.

"Are you feeling odd about me?" he asked.

Oh my God! Is he intuitive? I wondered.

As soon as I turned my face and looked at him, I felt so much peace and love in his eyes that I became speechless. Suddenly my mind was calm and I smiled. I wondered if I could be candid with him.

"What do you sense I'm feeling?" I choose to ask him instead.

"Well...you feel I'm a stranger. But I'm not," he said, and trying to convince me he went on, "We have known each other for a long time Lalla, just that you don't remember and I do. I am your friend and companion. You can be at ease and talk freely with me".

He calmed me down a bit, and made me feel more comfortable. Then he cracked a joke, and we both laughed to lighten up the situation.

I felt much better now, and could hold a conversation with him. Slowly I got used to his presence and got to know him better. I realized he was a very evolved soul, and more than just a companion for me. Perhaps I should be grateful for this transition. Let's see. Time would tell.

Chapter 12

Stories of Healing

In my session with Bonni, she had briefly mentioned that I would be experiencing some changes in the coming year. She had not given me much detail, and I didn't pursue it either as it wasn't my focus at that time. I was trying to understand what happened to Sid and spent many weeks adjusting to this new soul that Bonni said had replaced his original soul. Luckily, the Supreme, by some divine design, had placed a spiritual wife with him who could even relate to something like this, let alone deal with it. Amazingly he was able to carry on with his job as a neurosurgeon. I wondered about the secrets of this phenomenon. In the evenings this person, my husband, also started playing the part of guiding me spiritually. I used to listen to him in awe about the delicate intricacies and deep knowledge that is not available in books. Perhaps he gained this knowledge in other realms and brought them here on earth. This new soul in Sid's body seemed very evolved, and from my own insights I felt he was at the level of a master, or an advanced soul.

One night Sid easily and comfortably explained Bhakti, Shaivism, and Advaita in one go. I closed my eyes as he guided me to focus on my third eye and make my mind single pointed. In a few minutes I slipped into a thoughtless state called *Samadhi*. Sid watched me slip into this deep state, and then observed me for a couple of hours as I sat in bed oblivious to the outer world. He then rang a small bell from our altar, and I came out of this state slowly. My eyes were closed, but I was now conscious of my presence, and my mind was silent. Though my awareness was still in a higher realm.

I could 'see' (with my eyes closed) as though I was immersed in a brilliant light which was pulsating like a being. There seemed to be a healing and purification process on my soul by the light being in this higher realm. Then, what I identified as *Narayan* consciousness started descending from an astral plane into my physical body. After it filled this body, my awareness started to expand more and more, becoming the whole world, the sunset, clouds, space, stars, the galaxy, and further. There was a sense of unity and oneness. I felt different energetically as though I had become one with this *Narayan* consciousness that had descended into me while the body and personality of Lalla had become just a frame. As I looked within me, I saw my body had become golden light. I also saw a silver cord extending from that *Narayan* consciousness in the higher realm to my heart center. Perhaps as I was familiar with the Vedic beings I was being shown *Narayan*, a Christian may have seen Jesus or the Father in heaven.

"Lalla," Sid whispered softly.

I gently opened my eyes then looked at him and smiled.

"You went very deep," he said.

"Yes, it felt wonderful," I replied.

I told him what I had experienced, and he not only understood but explained it back to me. I got up to get some milk, then got ready for bed. There was still something different about me, I wasn't quite sure what it was.

◆◆

The world was slowly recovering out of COVID, and travel had started again. I had wanted my parents to come visit but didn't think it was still safe for them to travel. Abhi, his wife, and their one-year-old baby girl, Aditi, were brave enough to travel to India from the UK to be with family as it had been a long time. Though Abhi had serious mood swings and a strange unpredictable personality, he did care about our parents very much, and made sure he was there for them whenever they needed help. Perhaps the Indian family values got instilled in him deeply.

I could see my parents were getting older and it was hard for them to do physically taxing chores or big home projects or travel long distances. Abhi called me from Delhi and told me that he would like to take his company's offer to relocate to New York so that he could be in the same country as me and his children could also have better opportunities. In the long run he planned to settle in the United States, and as our parents aged, they could stay with him and me alternatively. I agreed with him and thanked him for thinking of the family.

For once we didn't get into an argument, though I had changed since our childhood conflicts. Anyway I would ignore or distance myself if he disagreed with me. I put forth my point in a detached manner and had no desire to prove myself, be right, or win the argument. Though I had to use more patience and skill to mold a situation. They were traveling to my parents during COVID, I wanted to make sure he and his family would isolate themselves for a few days in a hotel before potentially exposing mom and dad. If I had told him directly, he would have shut me down, so I had to use a male authority figure, being my dad and my doctor cousin, to talk sense into him. We lived in uncertain times, and we had to bond together as a family.

COVID brought a paradigm shift in the world in so many ways. People were fighting so many battles, and as I had won my own, I started to help others tackle theirs. There were issues with people not being able to meet each other with the lockdown, and on the reverse, there were relationship problems in families and couples who were locked in together.

A friend referred a woman, Sana, to me as she was looking for help in dealing with her husband. Sana, who was much older than me, was still quite traditional in her values even though they had come from Pakistan a long time ago. She worked in retail as her husband was irregular with his job due to his health and personality issues. They had two adult sons, one of whom was married with kids.

She sounded exasperated as she began venting the issues she was having with her husband for a long time which only became worse with him working from home because of the lockdown. He was moody, reactive, paranoid, unpredictable, had a big ego, and he would verbally abuse her very often for the smallest things. One day he would blame and dehumanize her, the next day he would show concern and care for her. To top it all off, he also had serious episodes of depression, where he would not come out of his room for days, and this was the main cause of his job losses. I understood very quickly that this man was probably bipolar, and displaced all the characteristics of one, including being a narcissist. My intuition also helped me 'see' through him, and gauge what was really going on. This was a sad and fearful man who had lost control over his emotions, and therefore threw fits of rage at the slightest provocation, with Sana being at the receiving end of his toxic outpouring.

I asked her, "Why do you still live with him? You have a job and can sustain yourself. If you choose to divorce him, you will also get fifty percent of the wealth. It would give you peace of mind and relieve you from this daily trauma".

Sana responded with, "I don't know Vinita ji, it would be very hard to live on my own, I've always been dependent on him for everything. He needs me too; I can't abandon him. He tends to become depressed, and I'm afraid his situation will become far worse if he's alone with no one to care for him. Also, it will be difficult for the children if our family is broken apart. Is there no way for him to improve, and become better? At least not so extreme in his temperament? I've heard you're intuitive, so may I ask you what you see for the future?"

Now this was very typical of most women I had spoken to. It was hard for them to let go and hard for them to live with an abusive husband. I gazed into empty space and asked within about what was to come. I could see her husband lying sick in bed, perhaps a hospital bed, with her and her son beside him. I felt it was about two years or so in the future.

I went on to say, "Umm, what I see is that he is going to be sick. It's not fatal, but I see him in bed unsold. I see you and your son beside him. I don't think he will change, but I think his emotional imbalance will lead to disease of some sort. It will probably be in about two years. But remember, time is elastic so I can't really say when. Also, this can change between now and then, as this is a probability or possibility as of this moment".

Sana reacted with concern, "Oh, will he be ok? He is not going to die, is he? What exactly will happen to him? I mean what illness?"

"I'm sorry Sana ji, I can't see the details, but it looks like it will not be a fatal illness. Not sure how long it would last. If I see any more, I will let you know. What is more important, is your own wellbeing. Your first responsibility is to take care of the body, mind, and life that Allah has given you, isn't it? You need to draw a boundary and not let him keep insulting you. This trauma will cause a lot of deep damage which takes years, if not lifetimes, to repair. So don't do this to yourself. Would you agree?"

Sana: "Yes absolutely, I agree, and it makes sense. But then how do I do it? I mean it's so hard for me not to interact with him or stay out of his way. I try so hard to do everything perfectly, and hardly speak in front of him. I'm so scared that I might do something wrong that he doesn't like and that's it, he will start shouting and yelling, and it terrifies me".

Me: "Again, my first suggestion to you is to leave him, and care for him remotely. Living in the same space as him, in that negative environment is not only difficult but also causing you harm. But, if you don't want to do that then you need to think of ways of either being out of the house, or in a separate part of the house. Perhaps you should also go to visit your family or friends alone for a few weeks in a year. You would have to be smart and think of options. I can only give you general guidance as giving specific logistical details may not be appropriate for your situation. Does that make sense?"

Sana: "Yes, I understand. I will try my best. Thank you so much for your guidance and help. I really appreciate it. May I call you again in the future if I need help?"

Me: "Yes of course you can! I hope things will get better, and like I said, take care of yourself first. I am glad I could be of some help to you".

Sana contacted me after a few months saying things were a little better after she started being mindful about her own wellbeing and creating more space between her husband and her. However; now there was another issue she wanted my advice on. So, problems never go away, they only change. We need to know how to deal with them. Also, it is very hard to change old impressions and patterns (*Vasanas*), it takes a lot of concerted effort repeatedly.

The Gita's methodology of Karm Yog, Bhakti Yog, Raj Yog and Jnan Yog is a perfect process to erase our *Vasanas*. With continued conscious practice we can rewire the brain, what is now called NeuroPlasticity. I had my own issues in life, and I found healers, etc. to help me. In this way we love and serve each other to learn and grow in this earth school.

——◆◆——

A person can respond to stress on body and mind in various ways, either with anger, depression, or anxiety. The most common complaint and cause of many diseases today is from stress. There was a friend's friend, Vishnu, who had a sudden onset of anxiety attacks. He was a young successful Indian American who had a leadership position at a startup in the bay area. Even though he was in good shape, did a lot of high mountain trekking, and was well grounded, he wasn't sure what set off this anxiety. It wasn't from work either, or was he having issues at home. Initially our common friend took him under his care.

As Vishnu's wife and children had gone off to his in-laws' house for several weeks during the summer, he couldn't sleep alone, and slept at our friend's place. His friend had them meditate daily. Still no help. Vishnu sought the help of many specialty doctors and got all tests possible, which found nothing. Anxiety doesn't show up in tests it seems, and must be clinically diagnosed, which it was. He started taking anti-anxiety pills along with a SSRI, which seemed to reduce the acute anxiety symptoms at least, but it was still significant.

After a few weeks, our common friend was off to India for about a month, so Vishnu started coming to me for help. When he first came, he gave me a history of incidents over the past year or so when he had felt some anxiety. The first time was when he had gone trekking in Leh, Ladakh (India). It's very high altitude, over eleven thousand feet, and one day he had trouble breathing, felt lightheaded, and had uneasiness in his chest. As they sent him down a couple of thousand feet, and gave him some altitude sickness medicine, he felt better the next day. However, when any such intense experience takes place, it creates a pattern in the brain and body to react in a certain way the next time a similar event takes place.

The next time he felt the same anxiety and altitude symptoms was when he went trekking later in the year to a mountain in Yosemite National Park that was over ten thousand feet. Again, the symptoms were short lived and became better overnight once he came down to lower altitude.

Then, a few weeks ago, he had an anxiety attack on a Disney Florida ride that took him and his kids through dark tunnels and was a mini roller coaster. He felt he had to get out of the vehicle, and wanted it to stop right away, but it couldn't. They had to wait till the ride finished. He managed to tolerate that discomfort by overpowering it, being distracted, and later by relaxing. The next day he had to take the flight home, while his family went off to his in-laws in a separate flight. On the flight from Orlando to San Francisco, he had a major panic attack. He thought he was having a heart attack and told the air hostess. Luckily there was a doctor and nurse on the plane, they took his vitals, and everything was normal, he just had a slightly elevated heart rate and BP, but the EKG didn't show a heart attack. Vishnu however insisted he was unwell and had to get off the plane, telling the pilot to return to Miami. Unfortunately, they couldn't do that, and gave him some antacid, telling him to relax. He couldn't sit in his seat, and felt better sitting on the toilet seat, so he sat there all the way to San Francisco!

When I looked into him intuitively, I felt his '*Vata*' element was sky high. As he was narrating this story, it triggered anxiety again. I gave him a couple of doses of homeopathic remedy Aconite 200, half hour apart, which calmed him down immediately. I advised him to go and see an Ayurvedic doctor at the Kerala Ayurveda center nearby in Milpitas, CA. Even though I was quite sure his Vata is severely out of balance, I wanted a doctor to examine him, and also guide him on how to bring it back into balance. In the meantime, I told him not to have any food that causes gas. I also helped him order homeopathic remedies, Stress Calm by Boiron, and Nerve Tonic by Hyland's. Later he told me that the Stress Calm was a life saver for him, and always carried it with him.

He came to me every day to talk, discuss, and I used to do intuitive counseling for him. I have seen that just listening to a person, and giving wise, appropriate advice relieves fifty percent of the issues. This I did free of charge, only as a service, which I'm afraid very few people do for others. One weekend I also did a regression session for him. Even though a couple of issues were released I felt there was more that needs to come out, and we were not done. As I got busy with something, I told him to go to a friend, Smita, to do another regression. She had done a regression session for me in the past as well. During the regression, something astonishing happened. When Smita regressed him to when he was in his mother's womb, she asked him to describe what was happening around him.

Vishnu: *"I see the family is doing some ceremony, everyone is wearing white clothes. It seems my paternal grandmother has just passed away, and they are doing the last rites. I am in my mother's womb"*.

Smita: "*Ok, tell me what happens next*".

Vishnu, after some silence: "*My grandmother's soul has entered my body*".

Smita: "*Oh! She entered the baby inside your mother's womb? And your soul is also there?*"

Vishnu: "*Yes, both of us are here*".

Smita: "*Is her soul still in your body even at the present time, which is now?*"

Vishnu: "*Yes, her soul is also present here*".

Smita then asked to speak to the grandmother's soul and asked her why she is in her grandson's body. His grandmother replied that she was very attached to her son, and it was hard to leave him as she was very attached to him.

"*But your son is now no more. Also, your being here in the same body is not good for your grandson*".

Smita then interacted with Vishnu's grandmother's soul to help her leave his body. The moment she did, Vishnu jerked up and fell back on the bed.

Smita: "*How do you feel now, Vishnu?*"

Vishnu: "*I feel lighter. I feel different. The energy within me seems different*".

Smita: "*Good, may your grandmother move on to higher realms where she will be more peaceful, and may you also heal after this release*".

Can you imagine that this can happen? His grandmother occupied his body along with his own soul for more than forty years! After the session, Smita and I compared notes, and we remarked how common it is for entities and other souls to use someone else's body. There can also be negative energy tentacles that can attach or interfere with one's energy body. After all we are first energy, then matter, and it's all about energy and vibrations. In Vishnu's case, maybe it was the grandmother's soul that was experiencing the anxiety and not him. Nevertheless, the body and mind had to be healed.

A combination of many healing modalities including allopathic medicines for about a month or two, the Ayurvedic remedies, homeopathic salts, lifestyle changes, as well as Pranayama and meditation got Vishnu to a point of some normalcy. He could now sleep for a few hours at night and go back to work.

Chapter 13

The Great Transition

So many people just around me needed healing from health, relationship, and financial problems. Mental health issues had become an epidemic.

I asked Sid, who performed brain surgeries, "Isn't it a fact that not enough attention is being paid to mind related illnesses?"

"A-ha. Yah, we have been paying attention to the physical side for a long time, but I think for the last decade at least I've seen a balance with mental health".

At least in the West people have recognized mental health problems and have stepped forward to address it. In many countries, most people are not educated or aware enough to distinguish between a personality trait and a mental or emotional imbalance. Mental health issues are also a big stigma in many cultures, and people hide it rather than seek treatment. If we don't accept a problem, how can we find solutions for it? I didn't necessarily believe in chemical-based medications for mental health disorders, as they have side effects, but for the short term they may be necessary. In the long run, the more society is open in addressing these psychological imbalances the more research can be put into finding better and safer treatments. For example, psychedelics have shown promising results in treating addictions and mental health problems.

I continued doing spiritual life work and guiding others. There were so many people with issues now and not enough healers or guides. I didn't feel adept at handling people with additions and referred them to other therapists and counselors who could. Marijuana had become legal in the US now, its use was widespread, and it was the new alcohol. Addictions are the other epidemic in society which are not being addressed in a systematic way. In the US, once someone is eighteen, they have the right to decide if they seek treatment or not. The family members or spouse has no rights to intervene in helping the person who may have a serious mental or personality disorder or severe addiction. Yet it is the family members who also suffer.

In India, it is still possible for family members, especially parents, no matter what the age of the person affected, to take this person for treatment. A change was needed in the US to have the family members be able to intervene and be given the rights to seek treatment for the affected person.

I started giving a lot of interviews on podcasts. People found out about me from my work. They were especially interested in my Vedic knowledge.

Like in one popular podcast I mentioned, "Most people are not aware of the nature of the mind. The default behavior of the mind ('*chit*') is to always flow towards the negative. Why expect it to be positive or pure? The world is like a video game in which the soul enters at birth with a body and mind. The whole challenge in this virtual reality is to guide the mind using wisdom from the Self. The symbolism of Krishna as the charioteer giving the Gita is of the senses as the wild horses, reigns as the mind, and Krishna holding the reigns symbolizes wisdom guiding the flow of thoughts. We must remember that we are not the mind and emotions. When we meditate, we can practice observing our thoughts, and realize that we are the witness consciousness. Everyone needs this knowledge to know how to manage our mind and emotions".

People had a lot of questions about understanding themselves, and needed clarity of knowledge on their own nature.

One person in our own family who needed guidance was Abhi.

Sunanda called mom to convey yet another crisis, "Mummy, Abhi just lost his job again. If he doesn't show up at work, obviously they are going to fire him," she said exasperated.

She was preparing dinner and Aditi, their little daughter, was crying in the background. Abhi couldn't hold jobs because of his addictions, mood swings and depression.

"I can't deal with this anymore! He gets drunk, then yells at me for plotting against him, it's so irrational," she continued breaking into a sob.

Poor Sunanda had to take the brunt of it, dealing with his narcissistic behavior.

"I have to manage his temperament, the home and also be both parents for Aditi," Sunanda now broke down into tears.

The problem is that Abhi wouldn't listen to anyone, except Sid sometimes. I kept requesting Sid to convince him on a treatment plan.

Sid shrugged his shoulders telling me, "Honestly, Abhi is…I would say delusional. He is in denial about his condition, keeps blaming external factors, and it is impossible to get through to him, Lalla".

After a few days we found out that Sunanda left him and went to her parents' place in India, taking Aditi with her. After my request, Sid mustered the courage to call Abhi again and he finally agreed on getting help.

Sunanda told my parents that she would not return till he took responsibility, acted on getting treatment, and showed improvement. I couldn't have spent more than a few days with him, his negative aura would have made me sick. I was surprised Sunanda stayed with him for so long. Honestly it is easier to help strangers than family.

Here at home, I helped who I could, I healed whoever came to me seeking relief. Sid also started taking interest in healing after seeing people being healed firsthand.

He told me, "You should document these as case studies, Lalla. Then I can perhaps help connect you with some doctors to certify these healings".

Though I wasn't so interested in an organized approach, Sid thought that there should be more structure to scale up, and these healings should be backed by science. I, however, looked at the spirituality behind the healing.

One lady from the Sri M group had invited me to her house to do a past life regression (PLR) for her. As she told me about her issues, I looked intuitively at where all this originated.

I started explaining to her, "What I've learnt is that a lot of our suffering from past experiences remains unprocessed in our subconscious or causal body, called *Kāran Sharir* in Vedic cosmology".

I could see intuitively that the current problem she described was coming from past lives, so I went on, "See...what happens is that repeated experiences leave layers upon layers of negative impressions, called *Vasanas*, in our subconscious mind. This causal layer of existence goes from lifetime to lifetime along with the soul. It is the cause of a lot of our psychosomatic health issues and illnesses".

I continued, "What PLR does is access the subconscious layer of the mind to release, process and resolve that suffering in a safe and healthy way. This could also be done through energy healing, plant medicine, psychedelics, hypnotherapy, theta healing, etc. Releasing these emotions that have remained suppressed for a long time brings a lot of relief and heals diseases or psychological disorders. Does that make sense?"

"Yes it does," she responded.

"Ok, so now let's start the PLR process".

I proceeded to guide her step by step through the regression session. She had a very powerful PLR and it accessed some of her past life impressions that explained some of her health and relationship issues with her husband. I told her that we would need another PLR to process more in a couple of months, in the meantime this PLR will start integrating into her life and she should tell me if she sees a change.

I thought that Sid himself was a natural healer being a very evolved soul and encouraged him to start healing people. So, Sid also learnt energy healing and started practicing it first with people he knew. He designed his own approach to healing where he created an integrative methodology which combined natural methods like yoga, alternative medicine like Ayurveda, as well as allopathic medicine when the illness was acute. As he was a surgeon, in his healing practice he became like a spiritual physician, giving people prescriptions of meditation, remedies for good sleep, herbs, nutrition, and educating them on a balanced life.

Being a Stanford neurosurgeon, more and more people started coming to him just via word of mouth. Sid also came to know a few other doctors who had alternate approaches to health and healing which helped him develop his approach as well. Both Sid and I often interacted with someone who came to us for help. I was good at giving wisdom and looking into the issue intuitively, while Sid was good at integrative remedies and solutions.

As we started hearing more and more stories, Sid and I realized that many people, especially those who grew up in America, had a lot of serious issues growing up like drugs, alcohol, sexual abuse from a family member, divorced parents, and a broken family structure. Too much use of technology and gadgets, peer pressure amongst the youth, and a very superficial social media culture had been affecting the youth for over a decade.

I personally felt that people were so disconnected from their soul, from each other, and with the Supreme. This I thought was the root cause of many psychological issues. As they didn't feel a sense of belonging, they were lost, confused, and didn't feel loved. Most people had superficial relationships, yet it is the human connection, the bonds of relationships, of sharing love, which feeds our essential life force. Without this we become like machines.

Those who were healthy and happy had good family support, some deep friendships. and felt connected to others. The ones who thrived experienced their own inner spirit in which they could anchor themselves, as well as have faith in that Supreme Being that does all the magic in creation.

Many people also didn't know who they really were. Once a very successful professional man, Ollie, had come to Sid and I for help with his anxiety and health issues as his doctor told him to look into meditation and alternative healing. Sid asked him to describe his feelings or what was bothering him. Ollie was unable to get in touch with his own feelings or identify what was the problem within.

Sid started explaining some basic knowledge, "Individuals usually identify with their body, mind and personality when defining who they are. They go with the flow of their thoughts and feelings, however unbeneficial or uncontrollable, and fall victim to their own lower nature. That's where the Yogic philosophy is extremely useful. Knowing the different layers of our existence, and our true identity as the eternal Self, gives us the ability to guide our lower nature. Body, breath, thinking faculty, discernment ability, memory, ego, and Self are briefly the layers of our existence. Are you with me so far?" Sid asked.

"Yes I think so," Ollie said, still a little unclear and they proceeded into a dialogue to explore his inner world.

Perhaps it is the compounding effect over many lifetimes that the souls present now were so damaged. It was the scarring of the soul with trauma, negative emotions, bad experiences, as well as the lack of healing or evolution that may have resulted in the massive amounts of psychological problems. We seemed to be at a breaking point as a human species. Even though medical advances were being made, the mind of most humans had become unhealthier, which then caused more distress. With so many people carrying tarnished energies, it had a compounding effect on humanity. The collective consciousness was now at an inflection point, and I was sure nature would bring in corrective measures to restore balance.

Not only did humans wound their souls, they had also damaged the Earth. In no other time in history have we depleted and destroyed the natural balance of the planet in such a short time. I know people talk about climate change being man-made, which is true, but the earth is also warming up due to precession of the equinoxes. The earth naturally goes through ice ages during cooling, and warm ages that last approximately thirteen thousand years each. Now we are seeing an acceleration of the combined effect of manmade and natural calamities. I was sure that if we stay on the current track which is unsustainable, we will only destroy ourselves and the planet. Perhaps the divine forces would intervene and change our course?

One day while Sid and I were out grocery shopping, we saw notifications on our mobile phones that there was a huge attack on Israel by terrorists. We came home and put on the news and were all shocked by the massacre. There was a huge reaction worldwide, and now humanity was even more divided than before. In the days that followed, I could sense the anger in conversations people were having, some of our friends argued, took sides, and grew distant from each other. I wondered if there was some dark design behind all this to divide communities.

About a month after the Hamas attack and a few days after a solar eclipse, Israel responded with a military invasion of Gaza. We were all expecting this, so it wasn't a surprise. It seemed like the whole world had moved from one crisis to the next. My first feeling when this happened was that this was the start of something bigger and an ominous sign of something destined for humanity in the years to come. Intuitively I saw missiles would be fired from Iran into Israel after the next solar eclipse in six months. I also felt there would be serious natural disasters this year as well. I felt really uneasy.

Something within me stirred, like some energy gurgling. In my meditations over several days, I saw some visions of vague events which I assumed were about the future. I felt a little uneasy and sought Sid's help. As I began to convey my visions to Sid, I started seeing them again with my eyes closing, this time with greater clarity. I felt the same *Narayan* consciousness get triggered within me, like a switch turned on, and it was this energy that spoke through me as I described the vision I was seeing.

First, I saw a huge Being standing in the Middle East, extending up into the sky. I could only see his legs extending into the sky and his giant feet placed over the entire Middle East. I don't know who that was, but it seemed like a Godly figure. Then I saw the entire Middle East being dug up into huge trenches deep into the earth. There was a gigantic angel in the sky, which I felt was

Archangel Michael. He had huge wings, and was flying over the Middle East. Then there was a violent whirlwind, like a sandstorm, churning the entire land and raising huge dust clouds.

After this everything settled down and became quiet. Henceforth I saw a large golden egg rising from the ground in the center of the Middle East, perhaps it was Jerusalem? In the sky above this golden egg, I saw a lot of angels singing and ushering in a new age. My voice changed a bit as I felt an exuberance about this transition. After this, there were ripples of ashes extending out from this golden egg, and this ripple extended around the globe till the whole world became ashes. From somewhere a new surface of the earth emerged, which looked like emerald green plasma. Sid intervened and asked what would happen to all the souls on the planet. I responded that they would migrate to other planets in the cosmos. We too would leave as we were here only for the transition. Sid asked what the timeline was for this, and I responded that it was in less than twenty years.

I ended this flow of information with a message, that we must not resist the change, that "Great power is needed for this transition, and we must allow this energy to work through us".

Once I finished speaking the energy within me also subsided. Sid and I talked a little bit. It was like something out of the Bible's chapter, Revelations. Sid had a feeling that I channeled this message, which could be true. I had to find out what exactly was happening to me.

I understood from this experience that my body is a divine vessel in which my soul, or higher Self, can reside. There was an archetype that I, and all of us, belong to. Perhaps it was the lineage of Lakshmi-Narayan that I belonged to. This is our soul's family tree, and through each member there runs the same energy.

With each additional experience, the energy world started becoming more important and prominent than just the physical projection. As our awareness expands, it includes the physical realm, but also extends to subtler realms. There were probably layers of veils that were removed one by one.

Meanwhile we watched as the world got torn by an escalation in the war. More countries were getting involved and taking opposite sides. Russia, China, Iran, Iran-backed militia groups like Hamas, Houthis, and Hezbollah organized themselves behind one another. On the opposing side, Israel, USA, UK, NATO, and most Christian countries lined up as a united front. Pakistan being a client state, funded by the US, was behind terror attacks in Iran. In turn Iran attacked Pakistan and started to control Pakistan's Balochistan province, cutting it off from Pakistan. Iran also started firing missiles at US air bases, and threatened attacks on Israel directly. The Houthis, backed by Iran, were attacking ships in the Red Sea making world trade dangerous and costly. These were the seeds of the next stage of this growing and expanding war.

———

Approximately six months after the war had started, which was soon after a solar eclipse, there was another solar eclipse.

"Lalla put on the news," Sid called me from work sounding disturbed.

"What happened?" I asked while washing the dishes.

"Iran has just attacked Israel…firing missiles! Just put on the news," he urged.

"Ok, ok. Bye".

I hung up the phone, wiped my hands and put on the news. As I watched the continuous firing of missiles and their interception exploding over the skies of Israel, it felt surreal, and if it was a replay of my vision, now in real life. I got goosebumps. My phone was buzzing with people trying to contact me as the news reached others. Even though there was minimal damage as the Israeli defense system obstructed almost all the missiles, this was a huge escalation and sent alarm bells all over the world. State leaders were nervous about the conflict spiraling out of control.

Unlike most of my spiritual friends who either disconnected their cable service or didn't watch the news, I did stay in touch just enough to be informed about geopolitics, but didn't get affected by it. So, Israel was not backing down, and was not even listening to the US State Department, which Israelis thought was compromised by Islamist-leaning officials. A few days after Iran's attack, Israel responded by striking potential nuclear sites in Iran, especially where it had secret underground facilities.

People were scared about a nuclear war, something I was almost certain the divine beings and evolved races would never let happen. I had also learnt that there were guard rails put on the extent to which we could use our free will, and a nuclear explosion was off limits. Things would mysteriously happen to defuse nuclear bombs, or other such adjustments. Was it time now for the 'ETs' to step in? I felt the time was close, and within a year or two they would make themselves visible.

"Hang on to my hand, you can do it!" yelled a firefighter holding onto a lady hanging by a cliff.

Another firefighter rushed to the spot with a ladder and rope and managed to rescue the lady.

"I need reinforcements here, fast!" said the firechief into a walkie talkie.

As if we didn't have enough rumblings in the world, we had a significant earthquake in the Los Angeles area a few months after the Iran-Israel conflict. It was 7.5 on the Richter scale. A whole row of homes dangled damaged over a hillside due to a rift followed by a landslide. There was mass panic and confusion everywhere. At least three flyovers had crashed, no one knew how many were dead. A couple of apartment buildings and high rises had floors collapse and people were trapped inside. Some roads were cracked, many houses, shops, and other structures had major damage. Cell phone service was jammed, there were gas leaks, and emergency services were really stretched. No one was prepared, and it was too late now to have an emergency kit and plan ready. The main problem was the lack of clean drinking water as many water mains were damaged.

Amazingly both Sid and I were calm, collected and reaching out to as many people as possible to pacify them. We organically started to organize help for people in southern California for those affected. Some Gurudwaras got into gear to serve food to those who lost their homes. Sid got in touch with a few temples to see if they could provide a temporary place for people to get shelter. I got in touch with the local Sri M Satsang group, and Chinmaya Mission where I knew people. Volunteers came together and quickly created relief packages to get delivered to southern California.

It would take several months of relief efforts, resettlement of displaced people, and repair of damaged structures before there could be some semblance of normality. Even before the west coast barely recovered from this major earthquake there was yet another catastrophic event on the east coast. A category five hurricane plummeted into Florida and then into North Carolina. There was massive flooding and damage along the pan handle. In North Carolina many trees came down which broke power lines and blocked roads. The federal emergency services, national guard, many non-profits, and relief agencies were stretched thin from two major disasters. International help was also coming in. Not to mention the major war going on in the Middle East.

Not to mention that this was also an election year for many countries in the world. America was more divided than ever before. Individual states were revolting against the federal power structure for their own rules around immigration and abortion. But there was one unprecedented event yet to come that would rattle America.

The Republican candidate was sentenced in a criminal case. We were not stupid, and realized this was politically motivated, so that they could label him as a 'convict'. As he could still contest elections, the Republican party nominated him as their candidate.

In October, just before the elections in November, there was a big bombshell when our old President, who was running for re-election, dropped unconscious on stage during a speech, live on TV. Sid and I watched the shockwaves reverberate throughout America and the whole world. There was so much uncertainty. Within a week it was declared that the current President can no longer serve as President, let alone run for re-election, due to his serious health condition. Our lame Vice President was now our President, ugh!

Now what? The Democratic party was scrambling for a replacement candidate via an instant primary, just weeks before the election! It was history in the making. People could not digest such news.

The US election was then postponed to mid December. The Republican candidate, who was a cult figure, won by a huge landslide. This re-elected President was also a divisive figure, people either loved or hated him intensely. Our country was being torn apart.

Only a few months after he took office, I got a WhatsApp text from a friend, 'US President shot, unclear if he's still alive'. Oh my God! Here we go again. I turned on the TV and watched CNN reporting that the President was shot at a public event, possibly being hit by two to three bullets. Two secret service agents were also seriously injured. He fell to the ground unconscious and was lifted by the secret service team and taken to the hospital in his bullet proof SUV. There was no official confirmation whether he was dead or alive. This happened about twenty minutes ago. I was trying to get through to Sid who may have been in the operating room. I checked the social media site, 'X', to see what the latest murmurs were there. A friend who was a political analyst on YouTube told me over text that most probably the President was no longer. That they will not release this information till there is an official and safe transfer of power to the Vice President who will probably address the nation. Stunned and confused I took a deep breath and switched off the TV. I didn't want any more craziness to be absorbed by my nervous system.

Sid finally called me and apparently it was all over the hospital, on every television screen. I couldn't believe we were witnessing this in our lifetimes. It seems as though the US was going through a political reset.

There had been too much to handle this year. I knew that this was the time for healers and spiritual workers to serve others in larger numbers. Those who had detached themselves and attached themselves to the unchanging permanent spirit, remained anchored in that which is Real.

——◆◆——

A few years went by with escalating tensions worldwide. We were now closing in towards the end of the decade, a decade of war and natural disasters. It was as though China was waiting for this opportunity when the United States was at its most vulnerable point. Many people were expecting China's invasion of Taiwan, which it claimed to be an integral part of China, under its One China policy. China's interest in Taiwan was mainly economic. As its own economy was at rock bottom, it was like an aggressive corporate takeover of Taiwan's semiconductor industry. An eternal enemy was also a good strategy to unite the people of China who were ready to revolt because of their economic woes. China was now on the verge of breaking apart into five separate independent states.

There were no intentions of an all-out war, as China wanted Taiwan's assets, not to destroy them. So, what China did was to create a blockade in the ocean around Taiwan. First, China used high-tech to create a complete internet blackout in Taiwan. Then, hundreds of Chinese ships and armored fishing boats encircled Taiwan, cutting off anyone going in or out. In addition to this, the Chinese air force surrounded Taiwan and created a fort in the sky. Many special forces and ground troops had already landed on the shores of Taiwan. Meanwhile the People's Liberation Army (PLA) Special Operations Forces (PLA Special Ops) had secretly entered the

Taiwanese parliament, the Presidential Office Building, and other government buildings.

No one really knew what was going on as the TV and radio stations were shut down. It had technology to jam radio signals and advanced weapons to crash Taiwanese planes and interfere with the equipment in the war ships as well. The PLA Special Ops had either assassinated or kidnapped the President and most of the cabinet, so there was no one to give orders. The Taiwanese army tried to resist and respond, but it was incapable of doing much with the speed and size of the Chinese aggression. In about two hours, the Chinese had overtaken the top brass of the government and some of the military generals. Then a Chinese army general made an announcement over national TV that China was now in control of the country, and that the Taiwanese leaders were in their possession.

The US had little time to take any decisive action to defend Taiwan. The sea barricade and air attack were in a way a diversion for the ground troops and special forces to get a free reign to take over. Over the next few months, the US and Chinese forces engaged in the South China sea around Taiwan. In the meantime, severe economic sanctions were placed on China that crippled its economy to a grinding halt. People were extremely fearful, and it spread like wildfire. It was obvious to most that we were now in World War III, because the US, Russia and

China were now involved in conflict. About six months later the US and its allies were finally able to overcome the Chinese forces and free Taiwan again. However, in the meantime the world's economy had taken a big hit. A majority of the people were living in fear and ego.

On the flip side in the spiritual world, Sid and I noticed that people were getting more established in their heart and listening to their inner voice. In our groups and communities, we watched the destruction, but moreover we saw the light replacing the darkness. With millions if not billions of people now spiritual, there was a myriad of responses, which ranged from predictions of doom and cataclysm, to mushrooming of self-sustaining communities. The spiritual community was abuzz with creating a separate reality.

Personally, I felt a flow of energy working through me, as I integrated my higher Self more and more into my presence, replacing my earlier personality as Lalla. Sid was like a lightworker on fire. He had stepped into his body already as an evolved soul and he was a leader, so people looked to him for guidance. In my spiritual community, more people started experiencing an elevation and expansion of conscious awareness.

The subtle astral seemed to open up like a veil being removed. Many people, including Sid and I, could now 'see' subtle beings of the astral realm, they always existed, yet we were not able to see them. As our vibrational frequency increased, we could see these non-physical beings in their realm, as our vibration now matched their frequency band. It's like tuning into a radio channel of a higher band and hearing what's being played there.

More incredible supernatural phenomenon was being reported. Many of my friends became intuitive. Healers were seeing more miraculous healings. The spiritual community was teeming with sensational channeled messages, and most people felt that we were on the brink of a shift 'event'.

I don't know if there was an energy shift, but things seemed to be racing towards a climax. Amid all the upheaval in the world, Abhi had moved to New Jersey and transferred his job to New York. My parents found it hard to cope alone, so they came over to live in the US for six months as a trial. They now had US residency and reduced their footprint in India. If living here with Abhi and me worked out, they would wind up things in India and move to the US permanently. I wasn't too sure if they would be happy here as they had no friends, nor daily routine like in India. Abhi's home environment wasn't very peaceful either with his strange temperament and unpleasantness with his wife Sunanda. It would also take a lot of effort for my parents to integrate at this stage of their lives.

Sid's parents were happy in India, and their daughter was a good support for them. They also had a large support structure there and were not interested in moving to the US. I had a deep sense that living in India would perhaps be better for all of us in the long run. Something I couldn't convince anyone of right now because my vision of the future didn't match the present state of things.

Chapter 14

Waves of Divine Light

"We seem to be in our own world Sid. It seems as though the negativity out there is not affecting us, and we seem to be watching it like a movie. Don't you feel that?" I said.

"Hmm," Sid looked at me pensively.

I continued, "And I also get a sense that they also don't seem to register us, or connect with, it's as though there is a split in humanity. Don't you think so?"

I was perplexed with this question and wanted to clarify my understanding with Sid.

"Yeah," Sid said, as his face brightened, "It's as though the split in humanity has become more prominent. I think, or rather feel, the ones who lean more towards spirituality, have risen in their energy level. So we have become invisible to those suffering from their own negativity".

Aha! I was not alone in sensing this. The ones who held purified and embodied values of love, forgiveness, service, knowledge, faith, humility, and so on, were gravitating towards higher states of consciousness.

I was told intuitively within me that we were first going to go through a phase of cleansing and healing. I personally felt light and grace purifying me during my meditations. Anything in my nature that finally needed to be cleansed was getting flushed out. There was healing I experienced that erased the wounds from many lifetimes. The ancestral baggage that was encoded in my genes (called *Pitra dosh* in Vedic understanding) also had to be released so that I would be free of that bondage. Sid had accumulated very little that needed to be removed from his etheric body. Though he too had to shed any layers of dust on the mirror of his soul. This cleansing was needed in the vessels for the flow of higher consciousness.

We seemed to have entered a magical world, there was perfect timing, and a flow of divine hand guiding it. Our close spiritual friends and communities were also feeling it. Everyone I talked to seemed to be experiencing a transformation and strange coincidences. Others' energies were also being purified. We saw light flushing out vapors of darkness leaving their subtle bodies.

Our Karm gets encoded into our genes or DNA. The genes we inherit carry energies from our ancestors which can influence us as well. Nature, environment and our behavioral choices can affect gene expression (epigenetics), and therefore our Karmic account. All the remnants that we ourselves did not remove through our learnings and evolution was now being cleansed by Grace and blessings from a divine force.

We heard many podcasts mention that all lifetimes had collapsed into the present, so we were living the Karm of all lifetimes in the present moment. It was a great time of cleansing and closure of unresolved desires and unfinished business from relationships. Those who had consumed and nullified most of the energy of Karm from all their previous births had a present net positive state and were healed. This was the prerequisite to receiving divine knowledge and unlocking our true potential.

We were like fish trapped in a net now freed to swim from the river to the ocean. All our gifts and abilities as multi-dimensional beings of consciousness were now available to us. Our third eye to see the subtle energies had opened.

People who held purer states of existence started separating from those who were addicted to negativity. We also saw a lot of suffering increasing in the world. It was hard to see close friends and family experience the repression of their limited existence. They just were not open to listening, we could just feel they were so unaware. What to do?

Those with a net negative balance from all lifetimes had to resolve heavy emotions or go through suffering. It was time to accept themselves, others, and situations as they are, rather than claim victimhood, or externalize the blame. Forgiveness also plays a big part in healing and moving on. Any remaining fear, anger, aggression, attachments, aversions, greed, selfishness, and other vices had to be confronted as this was a time of reckoning. Many of us who had gone through our own healing processes offered our unconditional loving help to those who were struggling and willing to learn, and some changed for the better.

In the business world, many companies were unable to sustain themselves with the huge worldwide recession as a result of the great war. There was mass unemployment, and governments were unable to give social benefits as they had no means to fund them. Masses of poor people were out of food and basic supplies, which led to a rise in organized retail crime, thefts, and rioting. Those who had borrowed large sums of money couldn't make payments to lending institutions. This led to banks going bust, which made people rush to the bank for cash. There is only a certain percentage of money that is paper cash in circulation, so this massive panic made the government take some extreme steps.

Within a year of the great war the US shifted to the digital dollar called, 'rWorld'. This Central Bank Digital

Currency (CBDC) was based on blockchain distributed ledger like the older cryptocurrencies. There were several CDBCs that were launched in the world, the one by China was the oldest, but there was now this new one launched by the US. There was a huge reset in the financial sector, one which caused a lot of confusion and fear. The massive recession and extreme federal debt were unsustainable, and the world knew that the fiat dollar was overvalued. The Federal Reserve had just kept printing dollars for too long. People were rushing to buy real estate, gold and other commodities whose prices went through the roof.

Six months after the digital dollar was introduced the US government suddenly devalued the dollar by lowering the cash value of the dollar by twenty percent. This meant that a hundred dollars was now worth eighty dollars. As we all had digital currencies in our accounts (like crypto) suddenly our bank account values were reduced by twenty percent by simply changing a number. The US dollar had been one of the key instruments of controlling the world, the price of petrol was pegged against the dollar, and all countries had to trade in dollars. This collapse of the world's reserve currency brought panic and fear, rumor and distrust across the globe. However; many countries had already shifted to multilateral trade in their own currencies. The ripple effect of this financial reset in the US was felt throughout the world. Several countries including India promoted their own gold backed digital currencies. As the borrowing power of the US had crashed it now had to rely on friendly countries to supply some basic commodities.

More and more spiritual people started leaving big cities to live in rural areas, like ranches or farmland, as the cities had become unsustainable. There was a rise in self-sustaining communities where people grew their own food, generated their own electricity (off-grid), and constructed their own water supply. These were modern villages that escaped from the crisis in the cities.

The Bay Area was no longer a place we could live in peace. There were massive shortages in power and water. This along with climate changing severely affected farming and increased wildfires. With more unemployment, crime had gone up so much it was no longer safe to live here. At night we would hear side shows in the intersection next to our condo. I didn't feel safe going shopping at night as there was so much retail crime, once it happened in front of my eyes while I was at the mall, the cops chasing a gang running with bags of clothes. Surreal, like a crime movie.

＊＊

The Bay Area had always been a double-edged sword of the material and spiritual, and now those distinctions were very evident. Sid and I decided to move to the outskirts of Colorado Springs where a group of our spiritual friends including Anu and Paul had joined a community and invited us. For now Sid took a sabbatical from his job to keep the door open to go back if our new adventure didn't work out. Our intuitions told us that Sid and I would split our time between the US and India. Right now Bharat was going through much turbulence and it would continue for another two years or so. When that settled is when more people would move to India.

Anu and Paul received us when we arrived at the community named, 'Center of Consciousness'. Paul introduced us to several folks after we moved in to our Pod and he gave us a tour.

"This is John, he's a musician, and Mary, his wife, is a great cook.

Hey Tina, come and meet my friends.

Tina is a healer. Here's Jordan, he's always busy building something. He's awesome! Helped us construct the cottages. His wife Tricia is a yoga teacher".

So in a few days we met more and more people. There was so much coherence here. The energy was amazing. In our dynamic community of one hundred and forty four (144) adults there was a perfect diversity of talent and roles.

Some had professional jobs before coming here and others were Shamans or healers. Several families belonged to the local area and were good with plant medicine. They were also useful as local guides for us to discover water and other resources. Many of our friends from the Bay Area also joined us here. It was an organic coming together of souls, as though by divine will. Our life here became connected to nature and spirit, as it truly should be.

We seemed to be in our element and comfortable in the flow of our activities here. I loved the Kirtan Satsang every evening after meditation at sunset. We felt pure love emanating from each one of us. There was no judgment between us. We could see energies as different colors emerging from people's hearts, minds or auras. Sid quickly became a good people organizer and leader and everyone loved talking to him.

Luckily our community had a good mix of teachers, builders, leaders, etc. We fit together as one like organs in a body. Each of us had community volunteer hours and we set up a school, kitchen, dining room, meditation hall, office, medical center, and various other necessities. Though we still went to Colorado Springs to get some supplies, for the most part we were self-sufficient. There was a shift in energy within the boundary of our community. It was like entering a bubble of peace. It appeared as though our communities were invisible to those with negative energy, they didn't seem interested or couldn't process the inputs of what they were seeing cognitively.

As our community started bonding, we realized that we were becoming telepathic. Initially we thought it was occasional but soon it became the norm. So, we had wireless communication like cell phones. I could think of my friend Anu for example, and she could be on the other side of our community doing something, but she would pick up my thought signals, and then send back a response through thought. We did talk also of course, but the thought communication held much more information and understanding than words. In our connection with each other there seemed to be a cord that connected us from our hearts. Even though we were all unique individuals we started to feel a sense of oneness, with love, as though we had a group consciousness. We were like a connected web of souls or like different parts of the same body. As we had been healed and purified there were no secrets, there was nothing to hide, and each one became translucent to each other. The other thing we noticed is that our physical body was also changing. Our bodies seemed to have reversed in age and healed from any diseases, so very little medical help was needed.

——◆◆——

The sun was emitting waves of higher consciousness energy in its solar storms as the current solar cycle started to become more active[1]. This was the first set of waves. It wasn't just physical sunlight and solar energy with its electromagnetic waves and radiation, but a higher consciousness which traveled on light waves and particles. One day a small group of us were parked on a bench outside the dining hut and chatting right after lunch. We were discussing this solar wave phenomenon which had lit up the spiritual world.

I told this group I was sitting with that, "What I have understood from the Vedic knowledge about the Sun, is that the Sun also has layers of existence just like we do. So, it has physical light, subtle light, causal light, and the light of consciousness also comes through the Sun. That's why the ancient culture of Bharat did oblations to the sun. In fact, the famous *Gayatri mantra* is addressed to *'Savitar'* which is the subtle form of Sun's light. Now if you look at the universe, the stars are portals through which cosmic consciousness shines into creation. They are a network of light in the universe. Like a black hole sucks energy into it, a star emits energy out, it may be two ends of a tunnel, entry and exit".

---

1. The sun goes through roughly a twelve (12) year cycle like a sine wave, with six years downward cycle, and six years upward cycle reaching a maximum for approximately two years.

Another person sitting on the bench also gave a quantum science equivalent, and equated it to quantum consciousness.

For those whose own consciousness and vibrations had risen, the sun's rays carrying consciousness became food or fuel, so we didn't feel the need to eat as much, as light became a source of energy for us. We felt lighter in weight and started seeing each other's bodies with more glow.

Even the sunlight had changed and the air was filled with more light than was clear as it usually is. The sunlight sparkled from tree leaves, grass, flowers, and even our hair and bodies. It was as though even the planet was changing from dense matter to lighter matter. The Earth became alive and so did the plants and animals. Most of us could feel and communicate with the subtle language of all sentient beings of which the planet was one. We could feel connected with Mother Earth, Gaia as some called it. It was the sun's rays and waves that were bringing about this change. We started embodying this Avatar consciousness.

On the other hand when we heard about people in the cities, they were almost burning up from the same energy coming from the sun. The ionosphere of the Earth was severely eroded, and all this radiation affected the satellites and communication systems. People holding lower vibration were not able to absorb and integrate this higher vibrational energy as their beings couldn't resonate with it. Dense matter and the physical human bodies were no longer suitable for this higher frequency light and environment of the new Earth.

The same electromagnetic radiation from the sun started causing massive cancers, nerve damage, brain disorders, mental health issues, and other diseases. People seemed to be aging faster, and many people were dying from illnesses. There was a huge rise in fear, anxiety, and psychosis in these people as they could not understand what was happening, and all they saw was death, disease, and disasters. People felt as though they were drowning and struggling to stay afloat. The fear of dying was overwhelming. Many were angry and violent perhaps as a coping mechanism in the hope to restore the normalcy they were used to. Others were depressed and could not accept that this was the new reality. People from conscious communities did their best to help those living in fear to give them a positive angle to the changes, give healing, or share knowledge and love. It is very difficult to detach and see the bigger picture in the face of death, unless one has the wisdom to attach to a higher reality.

A massive change was upon the planet, a cacophony of turmoil for most, a chorus of triumph for some. The tides of time brought endings to most, and birthing anew for some. For long we had borne the weary days now to bear the loving light for which we had come. The horizon of a new unfolding, of a new timeline, had arrived. Most had to face the falling of heavy structures no longer apt for the new reality, while some rose with the lotus blossoming from their heart towards the Source.

The descent of divine rhythms and tides was the culmination of choices we ourselves had made. Those who evolved to love collected together organically all over the globe. What was interesting is that many of the spiritual communities across the country and the world seemed to think and progress alike as though they could communicate with each other through thoughts or a deeper collective connection. The internet of consciousness. The Gaia center outside Boulder, Colorado became a main hub for collecting and dispersing information; it also started a daily news show. A few other spiritual centers/organizations became extremely important for communication and coordination for what was transpiring in the world. In addition to this some YouTube channels also became popular for us to hear others' experiences and understanding of what was happening and what was to follow.

An amazing and astounding discovery was made by a group of people from the east coast who were going to Bermuda via a cruise ship. One person on the deck ran to get his group of friends to show them what he saw. They all looked over the hull of the ship and not too far in the distance they saw an astral island. It was not solid, it was translucent, or seemed semi-solid. They could see the green shores, some organized building structures, and in the background they saw a huge pyramid that was shining bright. Soon many people gathered on the deck looking at this amazing sight. There were some psychics and clairvoyants on board who upon seeing this said that this was the missing Atlantis. It was there all along but we couldn't see it as it was on a higher octave. Now that our vibrations had risen, we could see it. Amazing!

Soon after, on the other side of the continent, in the Pacific, people saw Lumeria adjacent to Hawaii. There were small islands but most of them were water colonies.

Many exciting things were happening around us, however; part of my mind was also concerned about my family. I looked clairvoyantly first and saw different densities in all of them. Abhi was a dark dense color, my father was mixed, and my mother was mostly light. We invited them to live with us but they could not relate with what Sid and I were doing by leaving a cushy job at Stanford, a comfy home and going to live in a commune. Therefore, I went over to Abhi's place in New Jersey to be with my parents for a few weeks. It was so nice to be with them, especially my mother. When I arrived, she gave me the best tender loving embrace in the world. I took stock of their health. Abhi seemed very unstable mentally and emotionally. He was having headaches often. I told him to get his heart and brain checked as soon as possible. Sid also talked to him on the phone. I hoped he didn't have cancer as so many were getting. My father did get diagnosed with irregular heartbeat and high blood pressure. I got Ayurvedic herbs for Dad and Mom gave him homeopathic remedies. My mother seemed to be the most peaceful as she glowed like a queen angel. Such a lovely soul.

We talked about the issues in the world. The war and Earth changes with large and frequent earthquakes, tsunamis, hurricanes, devastating floods, wildfires, seasons changing, and these weird new solar flares. All these catastrophes were affecting farming, world trade, shipping, availability of freshwater, and the fundamental elements of survival were disrupted. All this fueling mass displacement of people. The east coast, which was more populated, had serious shortages, so people were going wild hoarding, and the shelves were empty everywhere. It was worse here than in Colorado where we had local food and supplies. People were in survival mode. We discussed what we could do in the long term as this situation just seemed to be getting worse. Living in New Jersey also had the danger of ocean water rising, or some other calamity. Abhi was adamant about staying here, at least for the near term. My parents were going back to India for the winter months anyway, so we could decide if they would come back the following year. I felt more relieved that they would be back in Bharat somehow, I felt that India would be more stable compared to other countries, in fact India was emerging as an anchor the world was looking for.

There were already large waves of people who had migrated to the US moving back to Bharat. Most of these folks were those who had lost their jobs due to the economic downturn. Many others were going back to be back with their families in India as they saw a lot of turmoil in the US, and the turbulence in the world caused a lot of instability. The deep-rooted family structure and extended family support in India brought solace to those who suffered from financial or health problems. India was still like a large village where everyone felt like family, or part of the close-knit community. A sense of belonging remained even after being weathered away from modern separation. One of the biggest problems in modern city societies was the breaking down of the family unit and the sense of community, as individuality and identity was stressed so much our feeling of connection has faded. This led to loneliness, suicides, and many other emotional issues due to lack of support, especially in times of trouble. That is why during COVID Indians and people in other countries with strong family ties fared much better than people in countries which stressed individuality, and where family structures had torn down.

———◆◆———

"It's not as rosy as you think Lalla. Living in the US you see only the good things about Bharat. Grass is always greener on the other side. It's different when you actually live here and face the day to day challenges," said my paternal uncle, *Pitar*, in India over the phone while I praised India.

"There are huge problems here too. You already know one big problem in India is that there are deep religious divides and still there are many communal riots of and on. Yah, of course most of them are fueled by political parties, they sacrifice people for power".

He agreed though that the current ruling party, however, served people well, put the country first, and was not corrupt for power or possessions. Many political leaders of India were genuinely working for the people's welfare, trying to bring harmony in India's vast diversity.

"*Pitar*, can I tell you what I feel? I think the most important aspect is that the government is protecting Dharm, and sustaining Bharat's ancient culture. Don't you think? It is also infusing people's sense of pride and self-confidence," I told my paternal uncle.

He mellowed down a bit and agreed. I think the pros were more than the cons now for Bharat.

Bharat's ruling party leaders refused to become puppets of western powers and did not bend to their arm twisting, or fall into geopolitical traps. India stood up to the enemies that were being created in its neighborhood by superpowers. The diminishing powers of the global elite were afraid of India's rise, and its authentic democracy. The global deep state did everything possible to corrupt various social leaders to destabilize and criticize the ruling party. China, Pakistan and a few other Muslim countries had tried and failed in attacking India through various overt and covert means. These countries were imploding and breaking up into pieces themselves. After the great war Tibet became a free country again and started a close partnership with Bharat, especially for security and economy. Tibet already shared an ancient spiritual connection.

India was now thriving. Indians had finally rejected the old colonial treatment by the West and overruled the illegitimacy of its faith planted by missionaries. Now the brown slaves were proud of their ancient culture, wisdom traditions, and Dharma based social systems. The arrogance of superiority and dominance by many countries was humbled and they could no longer oppose or ignore the luminosity of Bharat, the land of wisdom. Its leadership had gone through much hardship but consistently stuck to the path of Dharm. India gained the love, respect and gratitude of many people worldwide from Bharat's service to humanity. Wherever there were distress calls in the world, whether it was to rescue people from areas of war, or send relief, to give aid or loans, or to negotiate peace, everyone ran to the Indian government for help. Indian personnel helped humbly and unconditionally.

Many countries' heads learnt and looked upon the Indian leaders as mentors and guides. India had become the model country for the new world, emerging as the opposite of the dark immoral systems that were collapsing. This had not happened overnight. It took decades to cleanse the rotten system within India and struggling through establishing righteous systems while anti-national forces were trying to pull it down. With the dark forces losing power, finally the scales were tilting towards the establishment of a new Dharmic republic of Bharat. Many non-Indians also started coming to live in India as their own countries were close to collapse. Smaller countries in India's neighborhood requested India to make them satellite states giving them protection and prosperity.

Everything that resonated with love and service to others was being supported by a divine force. From the ashes of the fire of purification was rising the phoenix of divine will. Those who had come to hold the pillars of light, and anchor them into the Earth, had endured the tribulations, and risen from their slumber to embody the descent of divine light. The angels were pleased and singing in the skies while blessing the planet through this transformation.

Chapter 15

Coming of a New Age

I watched things happen before my eyes that I found astounding. Things I had heard and read about over a decade ago were coming true in some variation or another. One social system after another was being wiped out like a drawing board was being cleared, and slowly a new and better system was sprouting. The financial system, the pharmaceutical industry, the large corporate farming industry, the dependency on carbon fuels, health, education, and so many pillars of our society came crumbling down. It was hard for me and others to adjust to a crumbling of everything we took for granted and were conditioned to. In the long run it was good. We were moving from a highly regulated and controlled society to one that was governed by ethical and moral principles that benefited all and not just a few. The vertical pyramidical power structures we were used to, of the few controlling the many, came down like a house of cards. Now we were building horizontal models where we self governed and were humanity driven. But it was a very painful transition for most of us. However for those who had already moved into spiritual communities this transition was much easier as we were mostly incubated from the greater world and self-sufficient at least for fundamental things like food, water, housing, and energy.

"But Lalla I can't just drop everything and move back to India you know. You always have such crazy ideas! Aditi is in school. I know rent is sky high now, and I have to fight to find food to put on the table for my family. Right now I'm dealing with the crisis of having no health insurance like everyone else, so I can't even get my meds. It's all too stressful already, and you want me to think about uprooting everything and move to India!" Abhi ranted on the phone with me.

"But that's just what I am saying Abhi. It will be much more manageable if you are in India where care will be cheaper and you can stay with our parents so you don't have to pay rent, and there is more family support for all of you. Try to understand, I'm trying to help you".

I tried to reason with him patiently. Sid was sitting next to me reading a book, and looked at me from the side of his eye. It was pointless trying to help Abhi no matter how much compassion we approached him with, he just reacted with opposition and rudeness. His anxiety was driving him to become irrational.

Things were crazy everywhere. With public reaction to the societal breakdown, a lot of revelations became public as to how people were being controlled from the top by a few greedy and powerful families. Now it was time for this pyramid of control to be toppled from the bottom up. Humanity as a whole had to go through a cleansing process. So much time and opportunities were given to souls to shed vices of conflict, competition, ego, greed, and so on. When we do not purify ourselves then nature purifies us.

It was a very difficult time for me, my family, community and for all the people I saw suffering. It's easier said than done to go through a change of an age, a complete dissolution of what we had grown up with and been conditioned as 'normal'. What can we hang on to when even basic things that we took for granted were no longer available. It is hard to absorb emotionally. Like going to the ATM and withdrawing money was no longer normal. The natural disasters and economic collapse caused resource scarcity, and more and more people were unable to find or afford basic needs. Insurance for health and home was almost extinct now. Not only was our personal lives disrupted but there was a revolt against the corrupt powerful elite that treated people like slaves. People were on the streets, there was social unrest, and a huge rise in crime.

The situation in America, Europe, Middle East, Iran, Pakistan, Indonesia, and many other countries was now close to a civil war. Many states in America refused to listen to the Federal government and functioned independently. There was a seismic shift in the balance of wealth and power. India already had a stable economy, balanced resource distribution, and established in Dharmic values, it became a clear leader for humanity. The evil doers were being punished, and people felt safe, protected, and provided for by the government.

My parents stayed back in India more and more as they felt uprooted in the US, and Abhi's home environment wasn't peaceful or warm. Abhi had daily arguments with his wife, Sunanda, and she had filed for divorce. His health was getting worse day by day, in addition to the asthma that he had since childhood, we heard from his wife that he was also being treated for cancer. My mother was shocked and saddened. His unhealthy habits, his emotional imbalance, and negativity were to blame for the most part. Sid and I decided to go to India to spend some time with our families there.

People and things seemed so much calmer in India, but people were also more resilient to hardships. Many people had suddenly developed health issues related to the heart and also cancer. I'm sure the choking pollution and carcinogens in the food and water were a major contribution. I could barely eat anything and had to be very careful when I went out not to eat or drink anything. My uncle was right, India looked so much better from

America. It seemed as though it was a time for retribution or balancing of all our choices and actions.

On a collective level, a divine mechanism along with many evolved beings were slowly getting us ready for a quantum shift in consciousness. We were being introduced to a new reality, a non-physical dimension, step by step. Many souls had come here as volunteers to help mankind to move to a more evolved state of being. All these souls as well as those who chose to evolve from fear to love were now ready for this shift. As I myself had experienced some trailers of a higher vibrational state, as well as the descent of Narayan consciousness, so had everyone in our conscious community.

———◆◆———

Rig Veda:" There are beings on earth, in the sky, and in the waters. These beings live and function in ways that are hidden from us, influenced by divine forces and the cosmic order" (Rig Veda 10.90).

Bhagavata Purana:"*The universe is teeming with life, and many beings reside in planes that are beyond our sensory perception. These beings are part of the divine play and serve various roles in the cosmic order"* (Bhagavata Purana 2.2.41).

Many spiritual trailblazers like Dolores Cannon, movies like '*The Celestine Prophecy*', and evolved souls who had volunteered to come here, had described what was about to happen. However, as nothing like this had ever happened in human history, our conscious minds were not able to absorb or process this concept. If something bizarre like a spaceship and aliens are seen in real life, the mind becomes numb and the perception centers in the brain are unable to process the sensory inputs. Somehow for me and many spiritual people, there was a deeper knowing or some superconscious state that was familiar with extraterrestrial races, because once when I had seen an ET, I was not afraid at all and there was a part of me that was functioning normally with this ET.

Many reports started coming in mainstream media about UFO sightings. Initially there were a few. Slowly more and more people could see different types of spaceships in the sky. Some people recorded videos saying that they are getting telepathic messages from their star families (ET races) that it is time for them to return before the 'event'. By now all of us had sighted at least one UFO. One evening, while on a walk, Sid and I actually witnessed a UFO disk hovering over our community, and saw two slender, bluish skinned ETs entering one of our neighbors' homes. I did make eye contact with one of them, and felt a lot of peace and love emanating from him. That home belonged to an older couple, both of whom were sound healers, and were friends of ours. The ETs had perhaps come for a visit. Amazingly, I did not feel any fear at all. Such UFO landings were now becoming more common. Couldn't have imagined this would happen just a few years ago.

———◆◆———

In the year following the big war in Asia and many cataclysmic natural disasters, the solar cycle had reached its maximum like never before. Our community felt so disconnected with world politics. We humans were on the verge of destroying ourselves and the planet with nuclear weapons. This would not only affect the Earth but also the entire fabric of the solar system and beyond. On the other hand there seemed to be a divine design to intervene and erase the cancer growing on the planet using the hand of nature, and in our case, specifically the sun.

With the second set of solar waves there were more X-Class solar flares, and solar storms. This caused more earthquakes and volcanic eruptions. In addition to communication outages, there were prolonged internet breakages and disruptions to the power grid in the world. Again, those who had already established conscious communities were less affected, and they were guided on what to do, or how to prepare. We got divine messages that something was going to happen that would affect us.

This year there were a lot of water related disasters. To add to this there was a series of volcanic eruptions in Indonesia in October that affected the atmosphere worldwide. There was toxic gasses and volcanic ash released from this major earth rupture in the Indian ocean and Indonesia. Initially this was ignored by the western news media, but Indian and Asian news were reporting this as a potential threat. The volcanic ash gas clouds went up miles into the sky and spread in Asia. Then, as it continued it started heading for America and Europe. That's when the western news channels pressed the alarm bells and spread fear 24x7.

We were told to stay indoors, keep doors and windows shut tightly, recycle the air inside the house only, not to consume anything from outside, and wear gas masks if we had one (though you couldn't buy any and there were no deliveries) for a few days till the air shifted. Soon the effect of these dark gas clouds was so devastating it went dark during the day, the satellite signals were not getting through, there was mass chaos as communication world wide broke down. The whole world stood still in darkness for three days. As several clairvoyants and I also had seen this coming, most of the spiritual community had already prepared for this.

It was a huge cataclysmic event worldwide. There was so much shock and fear, many thought this was the end of the world. We had no idea what was happening in the world, but we knew and felt that thousands were dying. There were no phones or internet so I could only pray for my family. Sid had prepared his parents and siblings as well. We had to wait for three long days and longer nights. The earth rupture at the bottom of the ocean shore also caused large tidal waves, like a tsunami that swallowed the coastal regions of Indonesia, Bharat, Malaysia, Vietnam, and many islands were devastated. There was a large loss of lives, no one could even count. As I too knew about this, I had already had my whole family buy gas masks and had given them instructions on staying inside, and stocking up on food for three to four days at least.

Finally we were past it, and slowly life returned. Though there were massive amounts of deaths and cleanup of toxic areas had to be done. Again, this was a surreal experience. Many of these events were foretold by channel mediums, and I too had visions of these events long ago, so when I saw it in reality it seemed like a dream, surreal.

The solar energy seemed to also trigger a lot of spiritual people to experience a sort of high vibrational state. The sun was the feed through of cosmic consciousness, and solar ejections transmitted it to the solar system. There was a lot that the planet and physical bodies had to go through to rewire the DNA for higher frequencies and drop the lower density physicality. It was like the caterpillar losing its chrysalis to become a butterfly.

The birth of the light body emerging out of the physical structure was an unprecedented evolution into a new cosmic race. The masters who channeled messages through people, and the masters present on Earth, seemed to already know about this coming, and had spent most of their time preparing us to ascend. Spiritual leaders on the planet had formed support networks to help people understand what was happening to us, what was about to come, and also how to integrate this light energy. We had to graduate to the next stage of our soul evolution. All those souls that had come to the planet to help humanity through this shift in consciousness were in full gear as they knew the change within had been activated. So initially I had seen my light body in my meditations within me, sometimes when I was in an elevated state, like I felt vibrationally higher and lighter, I sensed that my body wasn't so solid and heavy. So the change for me was gradual. What we had heard about for so many years and been prepared for so long, had now become reality. This was it!

◆◆

The solar storms got more intense with each wave. In the third and final wave of solar storms, the souls whose bodies had been transforming over the last few years, migrated their awareness and consciousness to new light bodies. This was activated by the light codes carrying the information to activate the final etheric DNA (non-physical DNA), triggered by light, that completed the construction of the light body. The physical carbon based body and its DNA, burnt into ash by the solar radiation and fell away.

Sid and I also underwent this change from the physical to an etheric light body. We had gradually been changing over the years, but now we were permanently in this new body. The butterflies had emerged from the chrysalis. It wasn't strange, in fact I felt that this is who I really am, and always was, and that the biological body was my vehicle for me for so long for this moment, when I could finally emerge as my true self.

This solar wave carried with it a higher consciousness on a subtle level for our final shift. The souls that were chosen for this ascension could absorb these higher vibrations. They experienced a descent of Avatar consciousness, while their physical bodies disappeared. We could still see each other's subtle bodies which had a golden glow, like the angelic beings we had seen, wearing long flowy white robes and a halo of light around them.

The first person I could see now was Sid, he glowed and smiled like an ascended master. We could communicate telepathically, which was not words, but a multi-dimensional exchange of emotion, information, and understanding. Our bodies seemed to have become invisible for those who did not ascend, as we had split into two realities. We, however, could still see those who stayed behind in the old reality of physicality.

I could easily levitate and float above the ground then glide around wherever I wished. As I discovered I could move objects just by a wish. We could manifest whatever was needed immediately upon intending it. Like I wanted to learn how to temporarily change my form to the physical so someone could see me, and that knowledge appeared within me with visuals. The instant I thought of some place like my parent's home, or someone like my mother, that instant I was there, on the other side of the world, in my light body. It was all so magical.

What was amazing is that we could now see many beings, avatars and masters who already resided in this realm of higher vibrations. Each band of frequency is say a floor in a building, and everyone on that floor vibrates within that frequency band. When our vibration rises, we go to a higher floor of that building which already has other beings resonating with a higher frequency. The stories we had heard of the coming of an Avatar or Prophet seemed to be coming true in an opposite way. It is not that Kalki arrived or Jesus returned to Earth, it was they who waited to receive us as we ascended into a frequency which matched theirs.

It seemed intuitively as though some big extinction level event was imminent, and it was. A large solar vortex, like a firmament, erupted from the sun. This plasma energy, carrying high gamma wave radiation, was headed towards earth. This silent wave erased the earth's magnetic field and hit the earth like a large nuclear weapon shot from the sun. As the earth rotated, wherever the wave hit, turned into ash. Most of the surface of the earth became ash, and barely anyone survived. The ascended souls witnessed the mass extinction event taking place on the planet but as we were not physical beings anymore, we were not affected by it. Sid and I along with many others started floating up to the earth's atmosphere.

As I looked around I saw a stream of souls departing from the planet and flowing out into the solar system and beyond. In these souls, my mother came to me, she was at peace, as she smiled and embraced me with her love. My father also came and joined her, he too was at peace. They knew as souls that their mission to the planet was over.

After we said our goodbyes till we met again somewhere in some other plane, they floated off to their destination far away. I did not see any of my other relatives. Sid met his family in a similar way. Then Abhi came smiling, he could now return to his true nature as an evolved soul, his mission to enact the contract of duality with me was complete. The purpose of his life was to be a mirror to those who chose the dark side, and display the self destructive effects of their path. Abhi now returned to the higher dimension of souls in his soul group, and remained my soul friend. The earth was now clear of most of the souls that resided there for so long.

Then I felt an intuitive, telepathic, and energetic connection to a group of souls. These were the other 144,000, of which Sid and I were a part, and we became a collective consciousness, like a web of souls. It was time for us to do our job. I felt Sid's glowing energy form connected to mine on my right side. We and the others were linked with each other energetically forming a pattern like sacred geometry, just outside the earth's atmosphere. After we all got linked, we completed the circuit, and our vibrations became tenfold. At this time we opened the keys to the 144000 portals that we were all individually connected with. We had to all do this together else the portals would not open individually. Now the earth was able to receive the energies from the 144000 portals reopened. We then sent down our vibrations to the planet which became a temporary magnetic field or shield for the earth. Our role was to hold up the planet's vibrations, as its own magnetic field had been damaged from solar radiations. If we didn't do this the entire planet's vibrations would collapse and damage the earth. Our galactic family of 144,000 souls had come to the planet for this moment, as we were specialists in vibrations.

——◆◆——

I saw a plethora of spaceships of all shapes and sizes flood the earth, going to and from various places over the planet picking up souls that had ascended after completing their service in Earth's ascension. Those souls who had come for the shift, had done their jobs had now left on spaceships with their cosmic families. There were many Pleiadian starships that carried away the Pleiadian souls that had come to the planet, for example. These souls would now dorn Pleiadian bodies. There were other races as well, like the blue Arcturians, and so on. There was also a skirmish between some races, which I believe to be the light and dark races that were fighting over control of the planet. This was the moment when the dark races' reign was over, as the light races had come to play their part in transforming this living being, the Earth, to a higher vibrational non-physical planet.

Many categories of souls were seen busy with their roles in this momentous transition of our divine mother Earth. Masters, sages, as well as angels and Devas, led another group of beings coming in to help the earth move into a new reality. The top crust of the earth was burnt to ashes, and in some places it had turned over. It is like a snake changing its skin. The earth had lost its physical body and was birthing into a new baby planet. I saw the new earth as an emerald green pulsating energy that was still forming. A new group of beings were coming in who specialized in transitioning planets from one form to the birth of a new form, and then stabilizing it till it became habitable. All new beings and life forms that would come to this new higher dimensional planet would match its subtle density, and a new cycle would start again. In the spiral of time which is like a circular staircase, the Earth had now ascended to a higher rung.

Our guides and masters were now leaving as their roles here were complete. We also started departing with our soul groups. In this divine play we had concluded our act, and moved back into a realm beyond Earth's three dimensional space and linear time. Many adventures awaited us and many mysteries yet to be unraveled. Many creative impulses to be expressed, and many learnings through many experiences to be integrated for the soul to evolve. Never ending were these cycles within cycles of creation. Who knows whence it started, or if it ever did, and if the future was infinite or was this just the cosmic mind playing with time? Was this all an illusion, a projection, or a dream? As we evolved up the spiral towards the source, our souls merged into a collective super-soul in our next stage of evolution. An awareness that was expansive grew. Emancipation from a limited soul gave way to a realization that, '*All is One, I am that One... expressed as many*'. That One, blissful, wise, and infinite, expressing Itself through infinite forms to experience Itself, remaining just One. So let us joyfully join this divine dance of duality, and let the story continue…

"उदयाभासचर्वणलीलां विश्वस्य या करोत्यनिशम् ।
आनन्दभैरवीं तां विमर्शरूपामहं वन्दे ।।५।।"

मैं उस पूर्ण अहं विमर्श रूप आनन्दभैरवी को प्रणाम करता हूँ, जो इस सम्पूर्ण विश्व की सृष्टि, स्थिति तथा संहार रूप लीला लगातार करती रहती है ।

I bow to the Divine Mother *Parvati* who creates, maintains, and destroys this universe in her own Self. Inseparable from Siva, she is the blissful *ananda Bhairavi*. Filled with the inner awareness of her own nature, *Vimarsha*, she resides near the seat of her master, in the lotus of my heart.

Abhinavagupta. *Dehasta-devata-cakra Strotra* (the Divine Mother within).